Samuel French Acting Edition

Jane Austen's
Sense and Sensibility

Adapted by Emma Whipday
with Brian McMahon

SAMUELFRENCH.COM   SAMUELFRENCH.CO.UK

FOR PRODUCTION ENQUIRIES

UNITED STATES AND CANADA
Info@SamuelFrench.com
1-866-598-8449

UNITED KINGDOM AND EUROPE
Plays@SamuelFrench.co.uk
020-7255-4302

Each title is subject to availability from Samuel French, depending
upon country of performance. Please be aware that *SENSE AND
SENSIBILITY* may not be licensed by Samuel French in your territory.
Professional and amateur producers should contact the nearest Samuel
French office or licensing partner to verify availability.

MUSIC USE NOTE

Licensees are solely responsible for obtaining formal written permission from copyright owners to use copyrighted music in the performance of this play and are strongly cautioned to do so. If no such permission is obtained by the licensee, then the licensee must use only original music that the licensee owns and controls. Licensees are solely responsible and liable for all music clearances and shall indemnify the copyright owners of the play(s) and their licensing agent, Samuel French, against any costs, expenses, losses and liabilities arising from the use of music by licensees. Please contact the appropriate music licensing authority in your territory for the rights to any incidental music.

IMPORTANT BILLING AND CREDIT REQUIREMENTS

If you have obtained performance rights to this title, please refer to your licensing agreement for important billing and credit requirements.

SENSE AND SENSIBILITY was originally produced in Staunton, Virginia by the American Shakespeare Center on 1 September 2017. The director was Stephanie Holladay Earl, with costume design by Jenny McNee, choreography and movement by Stephanie Holladay Earl, fight direction by Patrick Earl, and original music composed by J.C. Long (music director) and Hilary Alexa Caldwell (assistant music director). Period songs were suggested by Oskar Cox Jensen. The stage manager and assistant director was Thomas J. Coppola, and the assistant stage manager and understudy was Kendra Emmett. The cast was as follows:

JOHN DASHWOOD...................................Josh Clark
MR. DASHWOOD..J.C. Long
ELINOR DASHWOOD...............................Ally Farzetta
MARIANNE DASHWOOD ....Constance Swain
MRS. DASHWOOD............................Annabelle Rollison
FANNY DASHWOOD ....Hilary Alexa Caldwell
EDWARD FERRARS ....Ronald Román-Meléndez
SIR JOHN MIDDLETON ....Mitchell McCollum
MRS. JENNINGS..................................Topher Embrey
COLONEL BRANDON ....Calder Shilling
JOHN WILLOUGHBY ....Kyle Powell
LUCY STEELE ....Hilary Alexa Caldwell

CHARACTERS

(in order of appearance)

JOHN DASHWOOD – A serious and somewhat conceited man in his early thirties, he likes to think well of himself, and is devoted to his wife, Fanny. Son to Mr. Dashwood; half-brother to Elinor and Marianne.

MR. DASHWOOD – A loving and careful man, now "old" and frail in his fifties. Husband to Mrs. Dashwood; father to John Dashwood by his first marriage, and to Elinor and Marianne by his second.

ELINOR DASHWOOD – Sensible, loving, and conscientious, at twenty-one, Elinor is steadfast in her affections and committed to doing her duty. Daughter of Mr. and Mrs. Dashwood, sister to Marianne, and half-sister to John.

MARIANNE DASHWOOD – Headstrong, affectionate, and impetuous, at seventeen, Marianne is convinced she knows everything about love, nature, and beauty. Daughter of Mr. and Mrs. Dashwood, sister to Elinor, and half-sister to John.

MRS. DASHWOOD – A warm-hearted and optimistic woman. At forty, she can still be as romantic and impetuous as Marianne. Mother to Elinor and Marianne; stepmother to John.

FANNY DASHWOOD – A narrow and determined woman in her late twenties, cool and elegant in her manner, passionate in her love of her family, and unyielding in her ambition for them.

EDWARD FERRARS – A diffident, sensitive man in his mid-twenties, he is shy in company, but can be warm, affectionate, and even witty on closer acquaintance.

SIR JOHN MIDDLETON – A friendly, hospitable man in his late thirties, he is gregarious and generous; he has few interests beyond gathering around him as many lively young people as possible. Mrs. Jennings' son-in-law (his wife is pregnant, and we do not see her).

MRS. JENNINGS – A warm-hearted, tactless woman in her late forties, she is widely described as vulgar, but is not ashamed of her humble social background, and is pleased to be rich because it enables her to share her fortune with others. Mother-in-law to Sir John.

COLONEL BRANDON – A gentleman, aged thirty-five. In Elinor's words, he is "a sensible man, well-bred, well-informed, of gentle address, and possessing an amiable heart."

JOHN WILLOUGHBY – A gentleman in his early twenties. Passionate, charming, wilful, affectionate, and selfish.

LUCY STEELE – In her early twenties, Lucy is, in Mrs. Jennings' words, "monstrous pretty," and she uses this to her advantage. She is conniving and manipulative; she is also impoverished, with only her charms to rely on, and determined to marry well, at any cost.

SETTING

The action takes place in Sussex, Devonshire, and London.

TIME

Set in the 1790s.

AUTHOR'S NOTE

Suggested Doubling

Mr. Dashwood can be doubled with Sir John Middleton, and Fanny
Dashwood can be doubled with Lucy Steele.

ACT I

Scene One

[MUSIC CUE "PARTING GLASS"]

(Norland Park.)

(From offstage comes a cry.)

MR. DASHWOOD. *(Offstage.)* John! John!

> *(There is a confused sound of doors opening and shutting, and of running feet.)*

JOHN. Father?

> *(Enter **JOHN**, in nightcap and nightgown, with a candle, at a run.)*

Father? Where are you?

> *(Enter **MR. DASHWOOD**, old and frail, in only his shirt, leaning heavily on a stick.)*
>
> *(**JOHN** rushes to his assistance.)*

Father! You should be in your bed.

(Calling.) Some help, here!

MR. DASHWOOD. *(Wheezing.)* John. I have been looking over my accounts. You know that I do not have long left.

JOHN. *(Distractedly.)* Hush, Father, do not speak of this. *(Calling.)* Help, ho!

MR. DASHWOOD. John, you must hear me now. You know this estate is entailed on you, as the son of my first wife. I can leave only what money I have of my own to your stepmother and sisters, and that is but little.

JOHN. You need not trouble yourself, Father –

MR. DASHWOOD. John, you must do something for them. You cannot leave them in distress. You must make them comfortable. Promise me.

JOHN. Father, you must rest.

MR. DASHWOOD. Promise me you shall assist them!

> (**MR. DASHWOOD** *begins to cough, gasping for breath.*)

> (*Enter* **ELINOR,** *at a run, closely followed by* **MARIANNE,** *both in their nightgowns.*)

ELINOR. Father.

MARIANNE. Oh, Father!

MR. DASHWOOD. (*In a hoarse whisper.*) Promise!

> (*Enter* **MRS. DASHWOOD,** *in her nightgown.*)

MRS. DASHWOOD. My love! What do you do from bed?

MR. DASHWOOD. Promise me!

JOHN. I promise.

> (**MR. DASHWOOD** *coughs again, bent in two.* **MRS. DASHWOOD** *rushes to embrace him.*)

MRS. DASHWOOD. (*Semi-hysterical.*) Oh, my love, my love!

MARIANNE. (*Also beginning to weep.*) Papa, Papa!

ELINOR. Papa, the doctor said you must rest. Come now. Come to your bed.

> (*She gently disentangles* **MRS. DASHWOOD** *and takes her father's arm.*)

JOHN. (*Taking his other arm.*) Elinor is right, Father.

ELINOR. Marianne, help Mama. Come, Papa.

> (*Exit* **ELINOR** *and* **JOHN,** *who support* **MR. DASHWOOD** *as they lead him offstage.*)

> (**MARIANNE,** *still weeping, follows, guiding their mother off.*)

MARIANNE. Oh Mama, will he never recover?

MRS. DASHWOOD. I fear he does not have long, dearest.

MARIANNE. No – it cannot be!

MRS. DASHWOOD. We must prepare ourselves, my darling. We must prepare ourselves for the worst. And then – what will become of us?

(Exit **MRS. DASHWOOD** *and* **MARIANNE.***)*

Scene Two

(A funeral march* is played. Enter **ELINOR** *with a white funeral wreath, which she hangs on a door. She wipes tears from her eyes before exiting.)*

(Enter **FANNY**, *dressed finely in black, looking over a thick, white document with approval.)*

(Enter **JOHN**, *fully dressed now, with a businesslike speed.)*

JOHN. The documents are signed, my dear. All the formal processes are complete.

FANNY. And your stepmother and sisters?

JOHN. I have told them they must look upon Norland Park as their own home for as long as they wish. Though we are now master and mistress of it, they must not feel the need to vacate it.

FANNY. Very generous.

JOHN. They will wish to look out their own place presently, I should imagine. But until they do so –

FANNY. I cannot imagine they will wish to remain here at Norland for long. They will find somewhere that better suits their means. A little cottage will be very snug – though I wonder at your father leaving them so much of the china and linen. Some of it is much finer than ours. They will hardly have need of it, in the kind of place they can afford.

JOHN. *(A little nervous.)* My dear, I have been considering –

FANNY. *(Severe.)* Yes, John?

JOHN. I believe I shall give my sisters a thousand pounds apiece.

FANNY. *(Faintly.)* Two thousand pounds?

---

*A license to produce *Sense and Sensibility* does not include a performance license for any third-party or copyrighted music. Licensees should create an original composition or use music in the public domain. For further information, please see Music Use Note on page 3.

JOHN. It is liberal and handsome, and will be enough to make them completely easy. I can spare so considerable a sum with very little inconvenience.

FANNY. It is liberal indeed! What brother on earth would do half so much for his sisters, even if *really* his sisters! And as it is – only half blood!

JOHN. It was my father's last request to me that I should assist his widow and daughters.

FANNY. He did not know what he was talking of, I dare say; ten to one he was light-headed at the time. Had he been in his right senses, he could not have thought of such a thing as begging you to give away half your fortune to your half-sisters!

JOHN. He did not stipulate for any particular sum, my dear Fanny; he only requested me to assist them, and make their situation more comfortable than it was in his power to do.

FANNY. Well, then, *let* something be done for them; but *that* something need not be two thousand pounds. Consider, that when the money is once parted with, it never can return. Your sisters will marry, and it will be gone forever.

JOHN. Perhaps, then, it would be better for all parties, if the sum were diminished one half. Five hundred pounds each would be a prodigious increase to their fortunes! They can hardly expect more.

FANNY. There is no knowing what they may expect; but the question is, what can you afford. Remember, they will have money on their mother's death – quite a comfortable amount.

JOHN. That is very true; I do not know whether it would be more advisable to do something for their mother while she lives, rather than for them – something of the annuity kind I mean. My sisters would feel the good effects of it as well as herself. A hundred a year would make them all perfectly comfortable.

FANNY. To be sure, it is better than parting with a thousand pounds at once. But, then, if Mrs. Dashwood should live fifteen years we should be completely taken in!

JOHN. Fifteen years! My dear Fanny, her life cannot be worth half that purchase.

FANNY. Certainly not; but if you observe, people always live forever when there is an annuity to be paid them; and she is very stout and healthy, and hardly forty. An annuity is a very serious business; it comes over and over every year, and there is no getting rid of it.

JOHN. And with a yearly allowance, they would only enlarge their style of living, and would not be sixpence the richer for it at the end of the year. A present of fifty pounds, now and then, will prevent their ever being distressed for money, and will, I think, be amply discharging my promise to my father.

FANNY. To be sure it will. Indeed, to say the truth, I am convinced within myself that your father had no idea of your giving them any money at all. I'll lay my life that he meant nothing more than sending them presents of fish and game, and so forth, whenever they are in season. They will have five hundred pounds a year amongst them as it is, and what on earth can three women want with more than that? They will live so cheap! They will have no carriage, no horses, and hardly any servants – only conceive how comfortable they will be! I am sure I cannot imagine how they will spend half of it. They will be much more able to give you something.

JOHN. Upon my word, I believe you are perfectly right.

> (Enter **MRS. DASHWOOD** *with* **MARIANNE**. *She makes as if to withdraw, but* **JOHN** *steps forward.*)

How do you do, Mother?

MRS. DASHWOOD. As well as can be expected, thank you, John.

FANNY. *(With chilly courtesy.)* I hope my husband has conveyed to you how welcome you are in our home.

(MRS. DASHWOOD, offended, nods her head, and MARIANNE turns away.)

JOHN. *(Embarrassed.)* Do stay as long as you like. Stay another month, longer –

FANNY. Though recollect John, my brother Edward arrives this afternoon, and my mother may visit soon –

MRS. DASHWOOD. We shall hope to inconvenience you for as short a time as possible.

(She bows in a tiny curtsey. JOHN and FANNY return the gesture and exit.)

MARIANNE. Wretched woman! Offering to permit us to stay in our own home! Threatening to turf us out for want of room, when it is barely a week since our father's funeral!

MRS. DASHWOOD. Indeed, I am at my wit's end! To leave Norland would be unthinkable, but the presence of that woman makes it prudent at least! I have seldom met a woman I more strongly disliked. What are we to do?

ELINOR. *(Offstage.)* Mama! Marianne!

(Enter ELINOR and EDWARD.)

Mama – you must permit me to present to you Fanny's brother, Mr. Edward Ferrars. Mr. Ferrars, my mother, Mrs. Dashwood, and my sister, Miss Marianne Dashwood.

EDWARD. Mrs. Dashwood, Miss Marianne.

MRS. DASHWOOD. *(With a curtsey, very cold.)* Mr. Ferrars.

(MARIANNE, turning away, gives a vague almost-curtsey.)

EDWARD. Please forgive me, madam, for trespassing on your hospitality at such a time. Had my mother not demanded that I carry messages to my sister, I should never have presumed to...

(He peters out, embarrassed.)

MRS. DASHWOOD. *(Gentler.)* Not at all, sir. You are welcome.

EDWARD. I must confess that I owe you a further debt of gratitude, madam. Your eldest daughter has kindly rescued me from your beautiful grounds. I arrived on horseback, but was tempted from the path by some fine trees, and was at risk of wandering amongst them until nightfall.

ELINOR. It is a winding way, and very easy to mistake.

EDWARD. You are kind – I am a stranger in these parts, and their beauties quite led me astray. I am very thankful to my deliverer.

(**EDWARD** *and* **ELINOR** *smile at one another.*)

MARIANNE. *(Her interest caught.)* You came by the wooded grove?

EDWARD. Indeed. I quite lost sight of the house amongst your beautiful trees.

MARIANNE. Did you ever see such scenery? I declare the countryside here to be among the most picturesque I can imagine! – Did you not find it so, Mr. Ferrars?

EDWARD. It exactly answers my idea of a fine country. The hills are steep, the woods seem full of good timber, and the valley looks comfortable and snug.

ELINOR. I am of your mind. I like a fine prospect, but not on picturesque principles. I do not like crooked, twisted, blasted trees.

EDWARD. You admire them much more if they are tall, straight, and flourishing?

ELINOR. Exactly!

EDWARD. I am precisely of your taste. I do not like ruined, tattered cottages. I have more pleasure in a snug farm-house than...than...

ELINOR. Than a watch-tower?

EDWARD. I fear I shall offend you by my want of taste, if we come to particulars. I shall call hills steep, which ought to be bold; surfaces strange and uncouth, which ought to be irregular and rugged; and distant objects out of sight, which ought only to be indistinct through the soft medium of a hazy atmosphere. I have little knowledge of the picturesque.

MARIANNE. I am afraid it is but too true, but why should you boast of it?

ELINOR. Marianne!

MRS. DASHWOOD. We cannot all feel as you do, dearest.
(*To* **EDWARD***.*) The country is indeed a fine one, and I am glad that you admire it.

(*Enter* **FANNY***.*)

FANNY. Edward! The servants did not tell me you had arrived.

EDWARD. Ah, Fanny – Miss Dashwood has just rescued me from losing myself in her grounds.

FANNY. Nonsense. The grounds are not so very extensive. You can hardly have been led astray.

EDWARD. I fear I should have been, had Miss Dashwood not discovered me. I am no woodsman!

FANNY. You must not inconvenience the Miss Dashwoods, Edward. I believe you have letters from my mother to convey to me.

EDWARD. But first –

FANNY. I understand they are of the upmost importance.

EDWARD. Yes, I –

FANNY. Come, Edward.

EDWARD. (*Awkward.*) Yes. Good day, Mrs. Dashwood, Miss Marianne – and...

(*He turns to* **ELINOR***, grave and sincere.*)

Thank you, Miss Dashwood.

(**ELINOR***, affected by Edward's thanks, says nothing, only looks.*)

(**EDWARD** *returns her look.* **FANNY***, proprietorial, takes him by the arm.*)

(*Exit* **EDWARD** *and* **FANNY***.*)

MRS. DASHWOOD. Well! It is enough to say that Mr. Ferrars is as unlike his sister as I can imagine a man may be.

It implies everything amiable. I am sure I love him already!

ELINOR. I think I shall like him, indeed, when I know a little more of him.

MRS. DASHWOOD. Like him! I can feel no sentiment of approbation inferior to love!

ELINOR. I may esteem him.

MRS. DASHWOOD. I have never yet known what it is to separate esteem and love.

ELINOR. Well, Mama, I will not dispute the point. And now, if you will excuse me, I...

(Exit **ELINOR**, *blushing.)*

MRS. DASHWOOD. Well. I am pleased, after all, at Fanny's untimely invitation. You look grave, Marianne – do you not approve of Mr. Ferrars?

MARIANNE. He is very amiable, and it seems that Elinor finds him pleasing. But yet – he is not the kind of young man – there is something wanting. His eyes want all that spirit, that fire, which at once announce virtue and intelligence. And besides all this, I am afraid he has no real taste. Mama, the more I know of the world, the more I am convinced that I shall never see a man whom I can really love. I require so much! He must have all Mr. Ferrars' virtues, and his person and manners must ornament his goodness with every possible charm.

MRS. DASHWOOD. Remember, my love, that you are but seventeen. It is yet too early in life to despair of such a happiness.

(She sees the wreath that **ELINOR** *laid there earlier in the scene, and picks it up.)*

Why should you be less fortunate than your mother? Your dear father was all I could wish, and we enjoyed many years of happiness...

(They exit, arm in arm, with the wreath.)

Scene Three

[MUSIC CUE "THE JOYS OF THE COUNTRY - F"]

(Spring becomes summer.)

(Enter **ELINOR** *and* **EDWARD**. *She carries a sketchpad and pencil, and he carries a low stool. She sits on it and begins to sketch the grounds, pointing out the beauties of their surroundings – though we cannot hear what she says. He kneels beside her, supposedly to watch what she draws and how, but more often to gaze at her face, which she pretends not to notice. Occasionally she attempts to make him take the pencil from her, but he refuses, and they laugh together.)*

(Enter **FANNY** *on the upper stage, looking down at them with concern.* **JOHN** *joins her. They whisper together.)*

(Enter **MRS. DASHWOOD** *and* **MARIANNE**, *arm in arm.* **MARIANNE** *has flowers in her hair. The music ceases.)*

MRS. DASHWOOD. In a few months, my dear Marianne, Elinor will in all probability be settled for life. We shall miss her; but *she* will be happy.

MARIANNE. Oh Mama, how shall we do without her?

MRS. DASHWOOD. My love, it will scarcely be a separation! You will gain a brother, a real, affectionate brother. I have the highest opinion in the world of Edward's heart.

(During the following lines **EDWARD** *spots* **JOHN** *and* **FANNY**. *He rises.* **FANNY** *shakes her head at him.* **ELINOR**, *seeing his face, rises also.)*

*(***EDWARD** *murmurs something, bows to her, and exits.)*

MARIANNE. I love Edward tenderly. But he has none of that passion which I should expect in the man who could seriously attach my sister. Music seems scarcely to attract him, and though he admires Elinor's drawings very much, it is not the admiration of a person who can understand their worth. He admires as a lover, not as a connoisseur. To satisfy me, those characters must be united. I could not be happy with a man whose taste did not in every point coincide with my own. He must enter into all my feelings; the same books, the same music must charm us both.

MRS. DASHWOOD. *(Spotting* **ELINOR.***)* Ah, he has gone. You must speak to her, Marianne. As her mother, I would not press her for a confidence she is slow in giving, but she must long for a confidante – as her sister, you can press her as I cannot.

>   *(Exit* **MRS. DASHWOOD. MARIANNE** *moves to* **ELINOR.***)*

MARIANNE. Elinor! How is your pupil? I find Edward delightful in every respect, but I think it such a shame that he should have no taste for drawing.

ELINOR. No taste for drawing! Why should you think so? He does not draw himself, indeed, but he has great pleasure in seeing the performances of other people, and I assure you he is by no means deficient in natural taste, though he has not had opportunities of improving it. Had he ever been in the way of learning, I think he would have drawn very well.

MARIANNE. Do not be offended, Elinor. I have not had so many opportunities of estimating the minute propensities of his mind, his inclinations and tastes, as you have; but I have the highest opinion in the world of his goodness and sense. I think him everything that is worthy and amiable.

ELINOR. I am sure that his dearest friends could not be dissatisfied with such commendation as that. Of his sense and his goodness, no one can, I think, be in doubt.

The excellence of his understanding can be concealed only by that shyness which too often keeps him silent. At first sight, his address is certainly not striking; and his person can hardly be called handsome, till the expression of his eyes, which are uncommonly good, and the general sweetness of his countenance, are perceived. At present, I know him so well, that I think him really handsome; or at least, almost so.

MARIANNE. I shall very soon think him handsome, Elinor, if I do not now, when you tell me to love him as a brother.

ELINOR. I do not attempt to deny that I think very highly of him – that I greatly esteem him, that I like him.

MARIANNE. Esteem him! Like him! Cold-hearted Elinor! Oh! Worse than cold-hearted! Ashamed of being otherwise. Use those words again, and I will leave this moment.

ELINOR. Believe my feelings to be stronger than I have declared; believe them, in short, to be such as his merit, and the suspicion – the hope – of his affection for me may warrant, without imprudence or folly. But farther than this you must not believe. I am by no means assured of his regard for me, and I am very much mistaken if Edward is not himself aware that there would be many difficulties in his way, if he were to wish to marry a woman who had not either a great fortune or high rank.

MARIANNE. And you really are not engaged to him! Yet it certainly will happen soon.

(*Re-enter* **MRS. DASHWOOD**, *waving a letter triumphantly.*)

MRS. DASHWOOD. A reprieve, my dears, at last! I find in this letter the offer of a situation! A cottage in the country, offered on very easy terms, belonging to a relation of mine, a gentleman of consequence and property in Devonshire – you, perhaps, remember him, Elinor – Sir John Middleton: a gentleman of rank!

ELINOR. I recall the name, Mama, but I don't think I have ever had the pleasure of Sir John Middleton's acquaintance.

MRS. DASHWOOD. I daresay you were too young to remember when you saw him last. Your poor father – God rest his soul – was always a great believer in the warmth of Sir John's nature – so unlike Fanny!

ELINOR. And how will you answer this letter, Mama?

MRS. DASHWOOD. Why, I have already written to Sir John accepting his proposal. It is on such good terms, my dears, and Sir John writes so well and *so* warmly.

ELINOR. When do we leave?

MRS. DASHWOOD. At the earliest opportunity.

(**ELINOR** *turns aside, distressed but stoical.*)

(*Enter* **EDWARD**, *unseen.*)

MARIANNE. Leave Norland? Dear, dear Norland? Oh happy house, could you know what I suffer in now viewing you from this spot, from where perhaps I may view you no more!

MRS. DASHWOOD. We shall soon be at home in Devonshire, my love.

EDWARD. Devonshire? Are you, indeed, going there?

MRS. DASHWOOD. Oh, Edward – yes, we are provided with a house, with the assistance of my cousin, Sir John Middleton.

EDWARD. (*Half to himself.*) Devonshire – so far from here.

MRS. DASHWOOD. It is but a cottage, but I hope to see many of my friends in it. If my friends find no difficulty in travelling so far to see me, I am sure I will find none in accommodating them. You will always be welcome at Barton, Edward.

EDWARD. (*Still shocked.*) Thank you.

MRS. DASHWOOD. (*Jubilant.*) And now I must break the news to Fanny!

(*Exit* **MRS. DASHWOOD.**)

(**EDWARD** *and* **ELINOR** *look at each other.*)

(**MARIANNE**, *tactful, turns to go.*)

MARIANNE. *(With a curtsey.)* We shall hope to see you soon at Barton, Edward.

> *(Exit MARIANNE.)*

EDWARD. I am so sorry to hear you are to leave us, Miss Dashwood.

ELINOR. As am I.

EDWARD. Devonshire is far indeed. It is considerable – it is a considerable distance.

ELINOR. Yet, as my mother said, we hope to entertain many friends. We hope the distance may not prove insurmountable to those who wish to see us.

EDWARD. It would take a far greater one to keep a true friend from you. Miss Dashwood – may I – may I perhaps – as a friend of the family, almost family myself – may I call you Elinor?

ELINOR. Of course! My mother and sister have addressed you as "Edward" for some weeks now. There need be no formality with me.

EDWARD. Elinor, I should like you to consider me as a friend. I should like to think – though perhaps I may never – that is, I should very much like to feel...

ELINOR. You may always rely on my friendship, Edward.

EDWARD. Thank you, Elinor. I...

> *(He takes her hand, holds her gaze for a moment, then appears to recollect himself.)*

Yes. Yes.

> *(He bows over her hand.)*

Good day, Miss Dashwood. I – farewell.

ELINOR. *(Astonished.)* Good day.

> *(Exit EDWARD, at speed. ELINOR looks after him.)*

Farewell, Edward. Who knows if we shall meet again.

> *(She looks about her.)*

ELINOR. And farewell, Norland. Farewell, well-known trees. Our going will not harm you. No leaf will decay, no branch will become motionless because we can observe you no longer. You will continue the same, unaware of the regret we feel in leaving you, and insensible of any change in those who walk under your shade. But who will remain to enjoy you?

(After a final gaze, exit **ELINOR.***)*

ACT II

Scene One

[MUSIC CUE "BARTON COTTAGE THEME"]

(Enter **MRS. DASHWOOD, ELINOR,** *and* **MARIANNE,** *newly arrived.)*

MRS. DASHWOOD. Three bedrooms and a garret. It is not what you have been used to, girls, I know. In comparison with Norland, it is poor and small indeed. But it is a snug little cottage – too small for our family, perhaps, but we will make ourselves tolerably comfortable for the present.

ELINOR. Indeed, Mama, it is compact and comfortable, and the situation of the house is good.

MARIANNE. This prospect is extensive – I can see all of the valley, the woods and the pastures, and just glimpse the country beyond! That is an ancient mansion, there. I wonder who owns it?

(Enter **SIR JOHN** *and* **MRS. JENNINGS.***)*

SIR JOHN. Mrs. Dashwood! Welcome to Barton Cottage! Miss Dashwood! – A sincere pleasure, believe me – Miss Marianne! How marvelous. Allow me to present my wife's mother, Mrs. Jennings.

MRS. JENNINGS. Delighted, delighted.

MRS. DASHWOOD. Sir John, we are so grateful to you for your many kindnesses.

SIR JOHN. Not at all, not at all. Mrs. Jennings and I have an earnest desire to be on the most sociable terms with our new neighbours.

MRS. JENNINGS. Indeed, indeed, the most sociable, the utmost sociable!

SIR JOHN. You must dine at Barton Park every day until you are better settled at home – no, I will brook no refusal!

MRS. JENNINGS. He will not, and neither shall I!

MRS. DASHWOOD. Thank you, you are –

SIR JOHN. No thanks, no thanks, you are family! And you must allow us to convey all your letters to the post, and I will not be denied the satisfaction of sending you my newspaper every day. Should you ever require a carriage, mine is at your command. Now, what can I do for you? How may I assist you?

MRS. DASHWOOD. Sir John, you have been much too kind in finding us this wonderful cottage, and we are so well settled already, that there is very little –

SIR JOHN. Nonsense, nonsense, my dear, you are family! Now, you must dine with us this evening. Our group is small – there are so few families hereabouts – but I shall be delighted to introduce you to my dear friend, Colonel Brandon.

MRS. JENNINGS. A fine gentleman, with a great estate at Delaford, though *(Whispering.)* with a sad past, a sad sad past.

MARIANNE. *(Not listening.)* Sir John?

SIR JOHN. Yes, my dear?

MARIANNE. Can you tell me who owns that ancient mansion, in that winding valley there?

SIR JOHN. That is Allenham, my dear. A fine seat, indeed, but the lady who resides there is elderly.

MRS. JENNINGS. Indeed, indeed, though she is of very good character, she is too infirm to mix with the world. A sad thought, to be shut up so from company. I couldn't abide it, myself!

SIR JOHN. Indeed, indeed, we require company at Barton! I am delighted to have my charming cousins settled so near! And you must oblige us with your company tonight, indeed you must –

MRS. JENNINGS. I wish we could rustle up some smart young men. I have lived to see both my daughters respectably married, and I am always anxious to get a good husband for every pretty girl.

MRS. DASHWOOD. *(Ignoring Mrs. Jennings.)* We should be delighted to join you for dinner this evening. You are very kind, sir.

SIR JOHN. And I am sure your daughters both have fine voices. I should be delighted if they would honour us with a song or two.

MRS. JENNINGS. Indeed, I have a new song here – *quite* new, from London, performed at a little theatre on the Strand – I have no voice, but perhaps your daughters might like to try it – I'm always pleased to hear fine music when I can get it.

ELINOR. We shall be happy to try, ma'am.

> *(**ELINOR** takes it from her, pulls **MARIANNE** with her, and they look over it together.)*

"The Joys of the Country." My sight reading is poor – how does it go, Marianne?

> *(**MARIANNE** hums a little.)*

> *(**ELINOR** begins to sing, and **MARIANNE** joins her for the chorus.)*

> *(As they sing, the scene changes behind them, as it becomes the evening's party at Barton Park.)*

Scene Two

[MUSIC CUE "THE JOYS OF THE COUNTRY – C"]

(**COLONEL BRANDON** *enters with stools and is introduced to* **MRS. DASHWOOD**. *The four sit and watch the performance, as* **ELINOR** *and* **MARIANNE**'s *singing improves through familiarity with the song.*)

ELINOR & MARIANNE.

LET BUCKS AND LET BLOODS TO PRAISE LONDON AGREE,
OH! THE JOYS OF THE COUNTRY, MY JEWEL, GIVE ME!
WHERE SWEET IS THE FLOW'R THAT THE MAY-BUSH ADORNS,
AND HOW CHARMING TO GATHER IT, BUT FOR THE THORNS:
WHERE WE WALK O'ER THE MOUNTAINS, WITH HEALTH OUR CHEEKS GLOWING,
AS WARM AS A TOAST, HONEY, WHEN IT EN'T SNOWING,
WHERE NATURE TO SMILE WHEN SHE JOYFUL INCLINES,
AND THE SUN CHARMS US ALL THE YEAR ROUND WHEN IT SHINES:

OH! THE MOUNTAINS, AND VALLEYS, AND BUSHES,
THE PIGS, AND THE SCREECH-OWLS, AND THRUSHES!
LET BLOODS AND LET BUCKS TO PRAISE LONDON AGREE,
OH! THE JOYS OF THE COUNTRY, MY JEWEL, FOR ME!

> (**MARIANNE** *throws down the sheet music.*)
>
> (*The auditors applaud.*)

MARIANNE. Oh come now, this is absurd.

ELINOR. (*Covering for her sister.*) It is difficult to do it justice with so little practice, though I'm sure we shall enjoy working on it.

MRS. DASHWOOD. Will you give us one of your favourites, Marianne?

> (**ELINOR** *takes a stool with the others.*)

(**MARIANNE** *begins to sing a sad, mournful tune.*)

(*As* **MARIANNE** *sings,* **COLONEL BRANDON**, *caught by the sweetness of her voice and manner, rises involuntarily from his seat and gazes at her.*)

[MUSIC CUE "BLACK-EY'D SUSAN – VOCAL"]

MARIANNE.

ALL IN THE DOWNS THE FLEET WAS MOORED,
THE STREAMERS WAVERED IN THE WIND,
WHEN BLACK EYED SUSAN CAME ON BOARD;
SAYING, "WHERE SHALL I MY TRUE-LOVE FIND?
TELL ME, YE JOVIAL SAILORS, TELL ME TRUE
IF MY SWEET WILLIAM, MY SWEET WILLIAM SAILS
    AMONG YOUR CREW."

THEN WILLIAM HIGH UPON THE YARD
ROCKED BY THE BILLOWS TO AND FRO,
SOON AS HER WELL-KNOWN VOICE HE HEARD
HE SIGHED, AND CAST HIS EYES BELOW:
THE CORD SLIDES SWIFTLY THROUGH HIS GLOWING
    HANDS,
AND QUICK AS LIGHTNING, QUICK AS LIGHTNING ON THE
    DECK HE STANDS.

'O, SUSAN, SUSAN, LOVELY DEAR,
MY VOWS SHALL EVER TRUE REMAIN;
LET ME KISS OFF THAT FALLING TEAR;
WE ONLY PART TO MEET AGAIN.
CHANGE AS YE LIST, YE WINDS; MY HEART SHALL BE
THE FAITHFUL COMPASS, FAITHFUL COMPASS THAT STILL
    POINTS TO THEE.

(*The song ends in applause.* **ELINOR** *steps forward to compliment her sister.*)

SIR JOHN. Brandon? Are you well? You look like a man in a dream!

BRANDON. (*Stretching his shoulder ostentatiously.*) A little rheumatism – a mere twinge – it is nothing.

> (*He sits again, and he and* **SIR JOHN** *begin to converse in low voices, while* **MRS. JENNINGS** *leans over to speak to* **MRS. DASHWOOD.**)

MRS. JENNINGS. Mrs. Dashwood, I am remarkably quick in the discovery of attachments, and I suspect that Colonel Brandon is very much in love with your daughter.

MRS. DASHWOOD. Colonel Brandon?

MRS. JENNINGS. He listened so attentively to Miss Marianne's song, that I am perfectly convinced of it. I have long been anxious to see Colonel Brandon well married. It will be an excellent match, for he is rich, and she is handsome.

> (*As* **MARIANNE** *and* **ELINOR** *approach them,* **MRS. JENNINGS** *takes her leave, with a pregnant glance at* **MRS. DASHWOOD.**)

MARIANNE. What did Mrs. Jennings want, Mama?

MRS. DASHWOOD. Only to discuss what she thinks to be Colonel Brandon's sincere attachment to you, my dear.

MARIANNE. (*Laughing.*) Colonel Brandon? Quite impossible.

MRS. DASHWOOD. Not at all. He is but five and thirty – a good age for a man to think seriously about marriage.

MARIANNE. Mama, you cannot deny the absurdity of the accusation. Colonel Brandon is certainly younger than Mrs. Jennings, but he is old enough to be *my* father; and if he were ever animated enough to be in love, must have long outlived every sensation of the kind. It is too ridiculous! When is a man to be safe from such wit, if age and infirmity will not protect him?

ELINOR. Infirmity! Do you call Colonel Brandon infirm?

MARIANNE. Did you not hear him complain of rheumatism?

ELINOR. A small twinge!

MRS. DASHWOOD. (*Laughing.*) My dearest child, at this rate, you must be in continual terror of *my* decay; and it must seem to you a miracle that my life has been extended to the advanced age of forty!

MARIANNE. Mama, you do not do me justice. I know very well that Colonel Brandon is not old enough to make his friends yet apprehensive of losing him in the course of nature. He may live twenty years longer. But thirty-five has nothing to do with matrimony.

ELINOR. Perhaps thirty-five and seventeen had better not have anything to do with matrimony together. But if there should by any chance happen to be a woman who is single at seven and twenty, I should not think Colonel Brandon's being thirty-five any objection to his marrying *her*.

MARIANNE. A woman of seven and twenty, can never hope to feel or inspire affection again, and if her home be uncomfortable, or her fortune small, I can suppose that she might bring herself to submit to the offices of a nurse, for the sake of the provision and security of a wife.

ELINOR. It would be impossible, I know, to convince you that a woman of seven and twenty could feel for a man of thirty-five anything near to love. But I must object to your dooming Colonel Brandon to the sick chamber, merely because he chanced to complain of a twinge in one of his shoulders! Had he only been in a violent fever, you would not have despised him half so much. Confess, Marianne. Is there not something interesting to you in the flushed cheek, the hollow eye, and the quick pulse of a fever?

MRS. JENNINGS. *(Catching the last few words.)* A fever! Who is ill? I know the very best cure for a fever –

MARIANNE. We were speaking of – of fiction, ma'am.

SIR JOHN. Ah! You are a family of readers!

ELINOR. *(Rescuing her sister.)* We have been reading the works of Shakespeare aloud. We are nearing the end of *Hamlet*.

BRANDON. A fine choice.

MARIANNE. Do you think so? I consider it the very worst of his works.

ELINOR. Marianne! How can you say such a thing?

MARIANNE. Because it strays so far from the realm of possibility. Gertrude loves Old Hamlet, but after his death, falls instantly in love with his brother. It's absurd.

ELINOR. I believe that is rather the point. Hamlet blames her for falling in love again so soon –

MARIANNE. But it's not a matter of timing. A second attachment like that shouldn't be possible, no matter how long after your first love has died. If you have truly loved once, how can it be possible to love again?

SIR JOHN. Well, well, this is all very fine, this literary chat, I feel vastly improved already, but we cannot spend the whole evening in it.

MRS. JENNINGS. A game, Sir John – we must play a game of consequences. You can discover many a young woman's secrets through a game of consequences.

MARIANNE. *(Rudely.)* Forgive me, I cannot abide consequences.

(An awkward pause.)

SIR JOHN. Then perhaps bridge? Come, come, Mrs. Jennings, you shall trounce me, I know.

MRS. JENNINGS. You must be my partner, Miss Marianne, in reparation for refusing me, and we shall best Sir John, indeed we shall!

SIR JOHN. *(Extending his arm to **MRS. DASHWOOD**.)* If you would, madam –

MRS. DASHWOOD. I should be delighted, Sir John.

SIR JOHN. I know you never play, Brandon, but perhaps Miss Dashwood could cut in –

ELINOR. Thank you, sir, but I am quite happy to abstain.

SIR JOHN. Not a bridge player, eh? Readers and not bridge players – my, my, a literary family, indeed, a literary family.

*(The four sit down to the bridge table, **MARIANNE** unwillingly, and begin to play, speaking at a murmur.)*

*(**COLONEL BRANDON** offers **ELINOR** his arm, and the two take a turn about the room together.)*

BRANDON. Sir John can be a little severe on literature, but he is a fine and generous man, and a gentleman in the truest sense of the word.

ELINOR. Indeed, he has been so good to us, and we are very grateful to him. You have been friends long?

BRANDON. For many, many years.

*(A pause. **COLONEL BRANDON** checks that they are out of earshot of the others, just as **MRS. JENNINGS** gives a loud cheer.)*

MRS. JENNINGS. I have you, sir, I have you!

BRANDON. Your sister, I understand, does not approve of second attachments.

ELINOR. *(In surprise.)* No, her opinions are all romantic. But how she contrives to think so without reflecting on the character of her own father, who had himself two wives, I know not. A few years will settle her opinions on the reasonable basis of common sense and observation.

BRANDON. And yet there is something so amiable in the prejudices of a young mind, that one is sorry to see them give way to the reception of more general opinions.

ELINOR. I cannot agree with you there. There are inconveniences attending such feelings as Marianne's.

BRANDON. Does your sister make no distinction in her objections against a second attachment? Or is it equally criminal in every body? Are those who have been disappointed in their first choice, from the perverseness of circumstances, to be single during the rest of their lives?

ELINOR. I only know that I never yet heard her admit any instance of a second attachment's being pardonable. I look forward to the total change of sentiments that maturity must bring.

BRANDON. No, no, do not desire it; for when the romantic refinements of a young mind are obliged to give way, how frequently are they succeeded by such opinions as are but too common, and too dangerous! I speak from experience. I once knew a lady who in temper and mind greatly resembled your sister, who thought and judged like her, but who from an enforced change – from a series of unfortunate circumstances...

(*He falls silent.*)

Forgive me, Miss Dashwood. Your sister is very lovely. Do not wish that she may alter.

MRS. JENNINGS. What do you two speak of over there? Of what are you whispering?

SIR JOHN. I can guess what they whisper – Brandon, have you spoiled your surprise so soon?

MRS. JENNINGS. Miss Dashwood has got it out of him, I'll wager.

ELINOR. Indeed, I –

MRS. JENNINGS. I cannot blame him! For it is such an excellent plan. There is to be a party of pleasure – a day in the grounds of Whitwell, the estate of Brandon's brother-in-law. There shall be sailing on the lake, travel in open carriages, the finest provisions – a complete party of pleasure!

SIR JOHN. The Colonel himself proposed it, to welcome your family to the neighbourhood.

MRS. DASHWOOD. Oh, Colonel, we shall be delighted.

ELINOR. You are too kind, indeed, Colonel!

BRANDON. It is a pleasure.

SIR JOHN. Next Saturday, then, Colonel?

BRANDON. Next Saturday.

[MUSIC CUE "THE JOYS OF THE COUNTRY – F"]

(*All bow, curtsey, and exit.*)

Scene Three

(We are at Barton Cottage. Enter **MARIANNE**
and **MRS. DASHWOOD***, arm in arm.)*

MARIANNE. Mama, I have an alarm on the subject of illness
which I cannot conceal from you. I am sure Edward
Ferrars is not well. We have now been here almost a
week, and yet he does not come. Nothing but real
indisposition could occasion this extraordinary delay.
What else can detain him at Norland?

MRS. DASHWOOD. I am sure you are mistaken. Had you any
idea of his coming so soon? I, certainly, had not and
nor, I think, does Elinor.

MARIANNE. How strange this is! What can be the meaning
of it! But the whole of their behaviour to each other has
been unaccountable! How cold, how composed were
their last adieus! And Elinor, in quitting Norland and
Edward, cried not as I did. Even now her self-command
is invariable. When is she dejected or melancholy?
When does she try to avoid society, or appear restless
and dissatisfied in it? I'm sure I can't explain it.

(Enter **ELINOR** *with a basket of sewing.)*

Not more needlework?

ELINOR. Can you think of a more profitable way to spend
our time, while the weather is so gloomy?

MARIANNE. Gloomy? Do you call it gloomy? There is not a
cloud in the sky.

ELINOR. I can see seven at least.

MRS. DASHWOOD. I think the outlook brightens.

MARIANNE. It does, I know it does. I shall walk down
the hill, towards that ancient mansion. Such a lovely,
deserted house – it has achieved a strong hold over my
imagination. I believe I saw it in my dreams last night.

ELINOR. Dreams have the advantage of avoiding ill weather.
Would it not be better to wait until later, when the
ground will be less damp?

MARIANNE. I cannot wait another minute. Is there a felicity in the world superiour to a lonely country walk? I shall walk at least two hours.

MRS. DASHWOOD. Turn back at once if it rains, my dear!

(*Exit* **MARIANNE.**)

(**MRS. DASHWOOD** *and* **ELINOR** *turn to their work.*)

ELINOR. I do worry for her, Mama.

MRS. DASHWOOD. I know that she has not your gravity, Elinor, but I think her enthusiasms will do her very little harm, and may do her some good. I was very like her as a girl, you know, and I cannot allow myself to dislike the very qualities that won me your father. Reserve can sometimes be as dangerous as enthusiasm.

(*Pause.*)

I wonder when we shall see Mr. Ferrars.

ELINOR. I do not know, Mama.

(*Pause.*)

(*Enter* **WILLOUGHBY**, *carrying* **MARIANNE.**)

MRS. DASHWOOD. Marianne! What has happened?

ELINOR. Here, let me help you.

WILLOUGHBY. Madam, I hope you will pardon the intrusion. I think this is your daughter? I am sorry to say that she tripped and fell, and I fear she may have bruised her ankle. As I was out hunting, I saw her fall, and hurried to her to offer my assistance.

MRS. DASHWOOD. We are most grateful to you!

MARIANNE. (*Shyly.*) Thank you, sir.

WILLOUGHBY. (*To* **MARIANNE.**) I am relieved to see you are not hurt.

(*To* **MRS. DASHWOOD.**) I must take my leave now, but I wonder if I might do myself the honour of calling on you at the earliest opportunity?

MRS. DASHWOOD. We shall expect you tomorrow!

WILLOUGHBY. I shall not disappoint.

(**WILLOUGHBY** *makes as if to exit.*)

MRS. DASHWOOD. *(Calling after him.)* Might we know to whom we are obliged?

WILLOUGHBY. *(Turning to face her.)* My name is Willoughby.

(*Exit* **WILLOUGHBY**.)

ELINOR. Hold her head up, Mama, help her to breathe – I need to look at this ankle.

MARIANNE. *(Faintly.)* Please, don't trouble yourself. I'm sure I shall be quite well again –

ELINOR. Lie still, Marianne.

(*Enter* **SIR JOHN**, *out of breath.*)

SIR JOHN. Mrs. Dashwood – I heard from the servant – came straightaway – dreadful business – how is she, Miss Dashwood?

ELINOR. I think she will be quite well, Sir John, though she may not walk on it for a good few days.

SIR JOHN. Perhaps I should ride for the doctor?

MARIANNE. No, please. I am quite well. That man who brought me home, where is he?

ELINOR. Mr. Willoughby. He left just now. We are to expect him tomorrow morning.

SIR JOHN. Willoughby! What, is *he* in the country? That *is* good news; I will ride over tomorrow, and ask him to dinner.

MRS. DASHWOOD. You know him then?

SIR JOHN. Know him! To be sure I do. Why, he is down here every year.

MRS. DASHWOOD. And what sort of a young man is he?

SIR JOHN. As good a kind of fellow as ever lived, I assure you. A very decent shot, and there is not a bolder rider in England.

MARIANNE. And is that all you can say for him? But what are his manners on more intimate acquaintance? What are his pursuits, his talents, and genius?

SIR JOHN. *(Puzzled.)* Upon my soul, I do not know much about him as to all *that*. But he is a pleasant, good-humoured fellow.

ELINOR. But who is he? Where does he come from? Has he a house here?

SIR JOHN. Indeed no! Mr. Willoughby has no property of his own in the country, but resides here only while visiting the old lady at Allenham, to whom he is related, and whose possessions he is to inherit.

MARIANNE. *(To herself.)* That ancient mansion...

SIR JOHN. Yes, yes, he is very well worth catching I can tell you, Miss Dashwood, and if I were you, I would not give him up to my younger sister, in spite of all this tumbling down hills. Miss Marianne must not expect to have all the men to herself. Brandon will be jealous, if she does not take care.

MRS. DASHWOOD. I do not believe that Mr. Willoughby will be incommoded by the attempts of either of *my* daughters towards what you call *catching* him. It is not an employment to which they have been brought up. Men are very safe with us, let them be ever so rich. But I am glad to find that he is a respectable young man.

SIR JOHN. He is as good a sort of fellow, I believe, as ever lived. I remember last Christmas at a little hop at the park, he danced from eight o'clock till four, without once sitting down.

MARIANNE. Did he indeed? That is what I like; that is what a young man ought to be. Whatever be his pursuits, his eagerness in them should know no moderation.

SIR JOHN. It sounds like you may very well set your cap at him, Miss Marianne! Aye, you will make conquests enough, I dare say, one way or other. Poor Brandon! He is quite smitten already, and he is very well worth setting your cap at, I can tell you, in spite of all this tumbling about and spraining of ankles.

(**SIR JOHN** *shakes his head and exits.*)

Scene Three

[MUSIC CUE "WILLOUGHBY'S THEME"]

(We see **WILLOUGHBY** *enter, bow, and sit by* **MARIANNE**. **MRS. DASHWOOD** *and* **ELINOR** *fetch seats and* The Dramatic Writings of Shakespeare *and also sit.* **WILLOUGHBY** *and* **MARIANNE** *read aloud, as the music ceases.)*

(They perform their roles convincingly – **WILLOUGHBY** *with charisma and some humour, and* **MARIANNE** *with passion and seriousness. Each uses their character as an excuse to speak passionately to the other, and has eyes for no one else.)*

WILLOUGHBY. *(As Macbeth.)* Methought I heard a voice cry
"Sleep no more!
Macbeth does murder sleep," the innocent sleep,
Sleep that knits up the ravell'd sleeve of care,
The death of each day's life, sore labour's bath,
Balm of hurt minds, great nature's second course,
Chief nourisher in life's feast –

MARIANNE. *(As Lady Macbeth.)* What do you mean?

WILLOUGHBY. *(As Macbeth.)* Still it cried "Sleep no more!"
to all the house:
"Glamis hath murder'd sleep, and therefore Cawdor
Shall sleep no more; Macbeth shall sleep no more."

MARIANNE. *(As Lady Macbeth.)* Who was it that thus cried?
Why, worthy thane,
You do unbend your noble strength, to think
So brainsickly of things. Go get some water,
And wash this filthy witness from your hand.
Why did you bring these daggers from the place?
They must lie there: go carry them; and smear
The sleepy grooms with blood.

WILLOUGHBY. *(As Macbeth.)* I'll go no more:

I am afraid to think what I have done;
Look on't again I dare not.

MARIANNE. *(As Lady Macbeth.)* Infirm of purpose!
Give me the daggers: the sleeping and the dead
Are but as pictures: 'tis the eye of childhood
That fears a painted devil. If he do bleed,
I'll gild the faces of the grooms withal;
For it must seem their guilt.

> (**WILLOUGHBY** *leads the others in applause for*
> **MARIANNE**.)

WILLOUGHBY. Bravo, Miss Marianne, bravo. I have never
spent a better morning – I believe we do the Scottish
play justice. And now, Mrs. Dashwood, I must take my
leave. I am engaged to visit Colonel Brandon for lunch,
and am already late – although the delay is a happy
one, for Marianne is the finest reader I have ever heard.

MARIANNE. You flatter me, Mr. Willoughby.

WILLOUGHBY. Not at all!

ELINOR. I did not know you were acquainted with Colonel
Brandon.

WILLOUGHBY. Indeed I am – more's the pity, I sometimes
think. Brandon is just the kind of man, whom everybody
speaks well of, and nobody cares about; whom all are
delighted to see, and nobody remembers to talk to.

MARIANNE. That is exactly what I think of him!

ELINOR. Do not boast of it, however, for it is injustice. He
is highly esteemed by all the family at the park, and I
never see him myself without taking pains to converse
with him.

WILLOUGHBY. That he is patronised by *you*, is certainly in
his favour; but as for the esteem of the others, it is a
reproach in itself. Who would submit to the indignity
of being approved by such a woman as Mrs. Jennings?

ELINOR. But perhaps the abuse of such people as yourself
and Marianne will make amends for the regard of
others. If their praise is censure, your censure may be

praise, for they are not more undiscerning, than you are prejudiced and unjust.

MARIANNE. In defence of your protégé, Elinor, you can even be saucy!

ELINOR. My protégé, as you call him, is a sensible man; and sense will always have attractions for me. Yes, Marianne, even in a man between thirty and forty. He has seen a great deal of the world, has been abroad, has read, and has a thinking mind. But why should you dislike him?

WILLOUGHBY. I do not dislike him. I consider him, on the contrary, as a very respectable man, who has everybody's good word, and nobody's notice; who has more money than he can spend, more time than he knows how to employ, and two new coats every year.

MARIANNE. Add to which, that he has neither genius, taste, nor spirit. That his understanding has no brilliancy, his feelings no ardour, and his voice no expression.

ELINOR. You decide on his imperfections so much on the strength of your own imagination, that the commendation I am able to give of him is comparatively cold and insipid. I can only pronounce him to be a sensible man, well-bred, well-informed, of gentle address, and, I believe, possessing an amiable heart.

WILLOUGHBY. Miss Dashwood, you are now using me unkindly. You are endeavouring to disarm me by reason, and to convince me against my will. But I have three unanswerable reasons for disliking Colonel Brandon: he threatened me with rain when I wanted it to be fine, he has found fault with the hanging of my curricle, and I cannot persuade him to buy my brown mare. I am ready to believe his character to be in other respects irreproachable – and in return for this acknowledgment, you cannot deny me the privilege of disliking him as much as ever. In the security of this privilege, I must confess I am indebted to him, for he has invited me to join your party of pleasure tomorrow.

MARIANNE. Oh, Willoughby! Are you to join us? It will be a fine morning indeed.

(**WILLOUGHBY** *takes her hand and bows over it, before addressing the company at large.*)

WILLOUGHBY. Till tomorrow, then.

MRS. DASHWOOD. Until tomorrow, Mr. Willoughby.

(*Exit* **WILLOUGHBY**.)

ELINOR. Well, Marianne, for one morning I think you have done pretty well. You have already ascertained Mr. Willoughby's opinion in almost every matter of importance. You have discussed all the plays of Shakespeare, and read half of *Macbeth* aloud. But how is your acquaintance to be long supported? You will soon have exhausted each favourite topic. Another meeting will suffice to explain his sentiments on the picturesque and second marriages, and then you can have nothing further to ask.

MARIANNE. Elinor! Is this fair? Is this just? But I see what you mean. I have been too much at my ease, too happy, too frank. I have erred against every notion of decorum; I have been open and sincere where I ought to have been reserved, spiritless, and dull. Had I talked only of the weather and the roads, and had I spoken only once in ten minutes, this reproach would have been spared.

MRS. DASHWOOD. My love, you must not be offended with Elinor – she was only in jest. I should scold her myself, if she were capable of wishing to check the delight of your conversation with our new friend.

ELINOR. Indeed, I think Mr. Willoughby a very proper young man of good abilities, quick imagination, lively spirits and open, affectionate manners. There is nothing in him to dislike – except, perhaps, a propensity to say a little too much of what he thinks on every occasion, without attention to persons or circumstances.

MARIANNE. Indeed you censure him unfairly! I am sure I never heard him say an ill-chosen word – and I have done nothing but listen to him all morning!

ELINOR. That I cannot dispute.

(*Exit* **ELINOR, MARIANNE,** *and* **MRS. DASHWOOD.**)

ACT III

Scene One

[MUSIC CUE "THE JOYS OF THE COUNTRY - F"]

(Barton Park.)

(Enter **MRS. DASHWOOD, ELINOR,** *and* **MARIANNE** *with bonnets and shawls, prepared for a picnic.)*

(Enter **MRS. JENNINGS,** *followed by* **WILLOUGHBY.)*

(WILLOUGHBY *immediately leads* **MARIANNE** *to the side and they whisper together.)*

MRS. JENNINGS. *(In a loud whisper.)* And are they yet engaged?

ELINOR. Engaged! What can lead you to suppose it?

MRS. JENNINGS. I am sure they must be so – or very nearly – for they are never seen but they are together – besides which, I am quite certain that he has got a lock of her hair!

MRS. DASHWOOD. Indeed!

MRS. JENNINGS. I saw him cut it off, just now. They were whispering and talking together as fast as could be, and he seemed to be begging something of her, and presently he took up her scissors and cut off a long lock of her hair. Then he kissed it, and folded it up in a piece of white paper; and put it into his pocket-book. I saw it through the drawing-room window. Now is not this evidence enough that they are to be married soon?

MRS. DASHWOOD. I will not believe it until I hear it from Marianne herself. They have only known each other a few days.

(Enter **SIR JOHN**, *perturbed.)*

SIR JOHN. What is the matter with Brandon? Where can he be? He is never late.

(Enter **BRANDON**, *harried and uncomfortable.)*

Why Brandon! I was quite beginning to give you up.

BRANDON. Forgive me, Sir John. I have had a most unexpected letter.

MRS. JENNINGS. No bad news, Colonel, I hope.

BRANDON. No, ma'am. It came from town, and is merely a letter of business.

MRS. JENNINGS. For a letter of business it has discomposed you terribly, Colonel. Come, come, this won't do; let us hear the truth of it.

MRS. DASHWOOD. My dear madam, recollect what you are saying.

BRANDON. *(To* **MRS. DASHWOOD**.*)* I am particularly sorry, ma'am, that I should receive this letter today, for it is on business which requires my immediate attendance in town.

MRS. JENNINGS. In town! What can you have to do in town at this time of year?

BRANDON. My own loss is great, in being obliged to leave so agreeable a party; but it is not in my power to delay my journey for one day!

MRS. JENNINGS. If you would but let us know what your business is, we might see whether it could be put off or not.

BRANDON. I cannot afford to lose one hour.

SIR JOHN. Well, there is no persuading you to change your mind, Brandon, I know of old, when once you are determined on anything. When will you come back again?

MRS. DASHWOOD. I hope we shall see you soon at Barton Cottage.

BRANDON. You are very obliging. But it is so uncertain when I may have it in my power to return, that I dare not engage for it at all.

SIR JOHN. Oh! He must and shall come back. If he is not here by the end of the week, I shall go after him.

MRS. JENNINGS. Aye, do so, Sir John, and then perhaps you may find out what his business is.

SIR JOHN. Are you sure you cannot accompany us to Whitwell?

BRANDON. I assure you it is not in my power.

(Turning to **ELINOR.***)* Is there no chance of my seeing you and your sister in town this winter, Miss Dashwood?

ELINOR. I am afraid, none at all.

BRANDON. Then I must bid you farewell for a longer time than I should wish to do. Good morning to you all.

(He leaves, accompanied by **SIR JOHN.***)*

MRS. JENNINGS. I can guess what his business is!

MRS. DASHWOOD. Can you, ma'am?

MRS. JENNINGS. Yes; it is about Miss Williams, I am sure.

MARIANNE. And who is Miss Williams?

MRS. JENNINGS. What! Don't you know who Miss Williams is? I am sure you must have heard of her before. She is a relation of the Colonel's, my dear; a very near relation. She is his natural daughter.

ELINOR. Indeed!

MRS. JENNINGS. Oh, yes; and as like him as she can stare. I dare say the Colonel will leave her all his fortune.

MRS. DASHWOOD. And is it generally known, Mrs. Jennings?

MRS. JENNINGS. Generally known? No indeed. As if such a thing could be generally known, about such a gentleman as the Colonel. But I have told you, I am most expert at discovering secrets. And Brandon's is not the only secret here!

MRS. JENNINGS. (*Turning to* **WILLOUGHBY**.) I have found you out, sir, in spite of all your tricks! I know where you spent the morning.

MARIANNE. (*Quickly.*) Where, pray?

WILLOUGHBY. Did not you know, that we – that Marianne and I – had been out riding in my curricle?

MRS. JENNINGS. Yes, yes, Mr. Impudence, I know that very well, and I was determined to find out *where* you had been to. I hope you like your house, Miss Marianne. It is a very large one, I know; and when I come to see you, I hope you will have new-furnished it.

WILLOUGHBY. As to that, Mrs. Jennings, the house in question is a family property. I merely wished to show Marianne around.

MRS. JENNINGS. Indeed! Come along with you now, Mr. Willoughby, let us borrow you from Miss Marianne a short while. We want to hear what you've been up to!

> (**MRS. JENNINGS** *leads* **MRS. DASHWOOD** *and* **WILLOUGHBY** *off – the latter looking extremely uncomfortable. They exit.*)

ELINOR. Mrs. Jennings really is an incorrigible gossip! To think of telling stories like that!

MARIANNE. Why? Do you imagine, Elinor, that we did not go there, or that we did not see the house? I never spent a pleasanter morning in my life.

ELINOR. I am afraid, Marianne, that the pleasantness of an employment does not always evince its propriety.

MARIANNE. On the contrary, nothing can be a stronger proof of it, Elinor; for if there had been any real impropriety in what I did, I should have been sensible of it at the time, for we always know when we are acting wrong, and with such a conviction I could have had no pleasure.

ELINOR. But, my dear Marianne, as it has already exposed you to some very impertinent remarks, do you not now begin to doubt the discretion of your own conduct?

MARIANNE. If the impertinent remarks of Mrs. Jennings are to be the proof of impropriety in conduct, we are all offending every moment of our lives. I value not her censure any more than I should do her commendation. I am not sensible of having done anything wrong. And you shall not think I have done so either, when you return from church tomorrow.

ELINOR. What can you mean?

MARIANNE. Only that Willoughby has asked to speak to me, while you are all at church – quite alone.

(Exit **MARIANNE**, *excited.* **ELINOR** *follows.)*

Scene Two

[MUSIC CUE "PARTING GLASS – SACRED"]

(Enter **ELINOR** *and* **MRS. DASHWOOD**, *as from church,* **ELINOR** *humming the tune.)*

ELINOR. Was it wise to leave them alone together, Mama?

MRS. DASHWOOD. Can you doubt it? I wonder if he is still here. Oh, I cannot wait to hear the news – how I shall congratulate myself, when I have two such sons-in-law as Edward and Willoughby!

ELINOR. Mama!

(A cry is heard offstage.)

(Enter **MARIANNE**, *running and weeping, closely followed by* **WILLOUGHBY**.)*

WILLOUGHBY. Marianne –

MARIANNE. No, no –

MRS. DASHWOOD. Dearest –

ELINOR. What on earth is the matter?

(Seeing them, **MARIANNE** *gives another wail and exits.)*

MRS. DASHWOOD. Mr. Willoughby, has something happened? Is she ill?

WILLOUGHBY. I hope not. Indeed it is I who may rather expect to be ill – for I am now suffering under a very heavy disappointment!

ELINOR. Disappointment?

WILLOUGHBY. Yes, for I am called away to London, on business.

MRS. DASHWOOD. To London! – And are you going this morning?

WILLOUGHBY. Almost this moment.

ELINOR. This business will not detain you from us long I hope?

WILLOUGHBY. You are very kind, but I have no idea of returning into Devonshire immediately. My visits here are never repeated within the twelvemonth.

MRS. DASHWOOD. For shame, Willoughby, can you wait for an invitation here?

WILLOUGHBY. You are too good.

(*Pause.*)

MRS. DASHWOOD. I have only to add, my dear Willoughby, that at Barton Cottage you will always be welcome.

WILLOUGHBY. My engagements at present, are of such a nature – that – I dare not flatter myself... It is folly to linger in this manner. I will not torment myself any longer by remaining among friends whose society it is now impossible for me to enjoy. Good day, Mrs. Dashwood.

(*Exit* **WILLOUGHBY**.)

ELINOR. This is very strange. So suddenly to be gone! It seems but the work of a moment. Can they have quarrelled? Why else should he have shown such unwillingness to accept your invitation here? The circumstances are somewhat suspicious.

MRS. DASHWOOD. Oh, Elinor, how incomprehensible are your feelings! You are resolved to think him blameable. What is it you suspect him of?

ELINOR. I can hardly tell myself. It may be proper to conceal their engagement – if they *are* engaged. But this is no excuse for their concealing it from *us*.

MRS. DASHWOOD. Concealing it from us! My dear child, do you accuse Willoughby and Marianne of concealment? This is strange indeed, when your eyes have been reproaching them every day for incautiousness.

ELINOR. I want no proof of their affection, but of their engagement I do. Why do you not ask Marianne at once whether she is engaged to Willoughby? From you, her mother, the question could not give offence. It would be the natural result of your affection for her.

MRS. DASHWOOD. I would not ask such a question for the world. Supposing it possible that they are not engaged, what distress would not such an inquiry inflict!

(*Enter* **MRS. JENNINGS**, *at speed.*)

MRS. JENNINGS. How do you do, my dears? And where is your sister, Miss Dashwood? I have such news – we are to London! And with a young lady, whom I have had the satisfaction of discovering to be my relation, a Miss Steele. Her manners are so civil, and she is in such raptures about meeting you.

ELINOR. Meeting us? But we have no plans to go to town, Mrs. Jennings.

MRS. JENNINGS. Not go to town! I shall be quite disappointed if you do not. I have the nicest house in the world for us, in Berkeley Street. You must come, indeed. I am sure I shall be very happy to chaperone you. I am come now in person to invite you. You will enjoy Lucy Steele so much – she is monstrous pretty, and so good humoured and agreeable. And she longs to see the Miss Dashwoods of all things, for she heard at Plymouth that you are the most beautiful creatures in the world.

ELINOR. Indeed?

MRS. JENNINGS. And I have told her it is all very true, and a great deal more. And she is your cousin, you know, after a fashion – you are Sir John's cousins, and she is mine, so you must be related.

(*Enter* **MARIANNE**, *tear-stained.*)

ELINOR. Thank you for your kind invitation, but I fear our mother cannot spare us.

MRS. DASHWOOD. Now, Elinor –

MRS. JENNINGS. Oh, Lord! I am sure your mother can spare you very well, and I *do* beg you will favour me with your company, for I've quite set my heart upon us going to London together.

MARIANNE. To London?

ELINOR. (*Attempting to assist* **MARIANNE**.) Tidy yourself, dearest.

MRS. JENNINGS. Indeed, Mrs. Dashwood, I am sure you will not object to it, for I've had such luck in getting my own children off my hands that you will think me a very fit person to have the charge of your daughters; and *(Turning to* **MARIANNE** *and* **ELINOR.***)* if I don't get at least one of you well married before I have done with you, it shall not be my fault. I shall speak a good word for you to all the young men, you may depend upon it.

MARIANNE. I thank you, ma'am, sincerely thank you. Your invitation has ensured my gratitude forever. It would give me the greatest pleasure to accept, but if my dear mother were to be made less happy, less comfortable by our absence, nothing should tempt me to leave her.

MRS. DASHWOOD. I am delighted with the plan, and it is what I should wish. I have a little plan of alteration for your bedrooms too, which may now be performed without any inconvenience to anyone. It is very right that you should go to town; I would have every young woman acquainted with the manners and amusements of London. I will have you both go – your objections are nonsensical.

MRS. JENNINGS. It is just as I knew it would be! We must look over your things my dears, and see what is to be made ready – there is so much to do!

(Exit **MRS. JENNINGS** *with* **MARIANNE.** **MRS. DASHWOOD** *goes to follow.)*

ELINOR. Mama, is this wise? After Mr. Willoughby's sudden disappearance, how should it look if she were to go on purpose to follow him?

MRS. DASHWOOD. Nonsense, my dear. She goes to London as a companion to our dear friend Mrs. Jennings. And if she should happen to see Willoughby there, I know he would be delighted to see her. You think too little of him – as always.

(Exit **MRS. DASHWOOD.***)*

*(***ELINOR***, concerned, slowly follows her off.)*

(Interval.)

ACT IV

Scene One

(We are at Mrs. Jennings' London residence in Berkeley Street.)

[MUSIC CUE "LONDON THEME"]

*(**LUCY STEELE** and **ELINOR** enter, curtsey to one another, and sit.)*

LUCY. And how did you like Devonshire, Miss Dashwood? Barton is a prodigious beautiful place, is it not?

ELINOR. It is, Miss Steele.

LUCY. I have heard Sir John admire it excessively.

ELINOR. I think everyone must admire it who ever saw the place.

(Pause.)

LUCY. I am pleased Mrs. Jennings is delayed, Miss Dashwood. I was hoping for a moment alone, for I have something to ask you. I hope you will forgive the directness, as we have only just met, but I feel instinctively that you will understand.

ELINOR. I will render such assistance as I may.

LUCY. You will think my question an odd one, I dare say, but pray, are you personally acquainted with your sister-in-law's mother, Mrs. Ferrars?

ELINOR. I have never met her.

LUCY. Indeed! I wonder at that, for I thought you must have seen her. Then, perhaps, you cannot tell me what sort of a woman she is?

ELINOR. No, I know nothing of her.

LUCY. I am sure you think me very strange, for inquiring about her in such a way, and I am sure I should not have the smallest fear of trusting *you*; indeed, I should be very glad of your advice on how to manage in such an uncomfortable situation as I am; but, however, there is no occasion to trouble *you*. I am sorry you do not happen to know Mrs. Ferrars.

ELINOR. I am sorry I do not, if it could be of any use to you to know my opinion of her. But I never understood that you were at all connected with that family, and therefore I am a little surprised at so serious an inquiry into her character.

LUCY. If I dared tell you all, you would not be so much surprised. Mrs. Ferrars is certainly nothing to me at present – but the time *may* come when we may be very intimately connected.

ELINOR. Good heavens! What do you mean? Are you acquainted with her younger son, Mr. Robert Ferrars?

LUCY. No, not with Mr. *Robert* Ferrars – I never saw him in my life, and I hear he is a great coxcomb, and too silly for words. No, I speak of his eldest brother, Edward.

ELINOR. Oh.

LUCY. You may well be surprised, for I dare say he never dropped the smallest hint of it to you or any of your family; because it was always meant to be a great secret. I never should have mentioned it to you, if I had not felt the greatest dependence in the world upon your secrecy. Mr. Ferrars cannot be displeased, when he knows I have trusted you, because I know he has the highest opinion in the world of all your family, and looks upon you yourself quite as his own sister.

    (Pause.)

ELINOR. *(Faintly.)* May I ask if your engagement is of long standing?

LUCY. We have been engaged these four years.

ELINOR. Four years!

LUCY. Yes.

ELINOR. I did not know that you were even acquainted.

LUCY. He was four years with my uncle, who lives at Longstaple, near Plymouth. I often stayed with my uncle, and it was there our engagement was formed. You must have seen enough of Edward to be sensible that he is very capable of making a woman sincerely attached to him.

ELINOR. Yes... Engaged to Mr. Edward Ferrars! I confess myself so totally surprised at what you tell me, that really – I beg your pardon; but surely there must be some mistake of person or name. We cannot mean the same Mr. Ferrars.

LUCY. We can mean no other. Mr. Edward Ferrars, the eldest son of Mrs. Ferrars, of Park Street.

ELINOR. It is strange that I should never have heard him even mention your name.

LUCY. No; considering our situation, it was not strange. Our first care has been to keep the matter secret, for his mother would never allow the match. She believes Edward is likely to become very famous, and would never consider me suitable. I am sure I have no doubt in the world of your faithfully keeping this secret, because you must know of what importance it is to us, not to have it reach his mother.

ELINOR. I certainly did not seek your confidence, but your secret is safe with me.

LUCY. *(Wiping her eyes.)* Sometimes I wonder whether it would not be better for us both to break off the matter entirely. But then at other times I have not resolution enough for it. I cannot bear the thought of making him so miserable. What would you advise me to do in such a case, Miss Dashwood?

ELINOR. Pardon me, but I can give you no advice under such circumstances. Your own judgement must direct you.

LUCY. You are right, of course. Thank you, Miss Dashwood – Elinor. You cannot imagine the good you have done me.

(*Enter* **MRS. JENNINGS**.)

MRS. JENNINGS. Come, come my dears – I beg your pardon for keeping you waiting so long, but I have been forced to look about me a little, and settle my matters – Lord, I have been busy as a bee all morning! But now, we may at last head out and make our purchases.

ELINOR. I'm afraid Marianne is not yet ready. Perhaps I might remain behind, to wait for her?

MRS. JENNINGS. Of course, of course! But Lucy and I must brook no further delay – the shops will not wait!

LUCY. I have so enjoyed our little talk, Elinor.

(*Exit* **LUCY** *and* **MRS. JENNINGS**.)

(**ELINOR** *sits, shocked.*)

(*Enter* **MARIANNE**.)

MARIANNE. Have they gone at last?

(*She runs to the window.*)

Yes, I see them crossing the street. I hope they may be gone all day!

ELINOR. Really, Marianne, you cannot avoid them forever. Mrs. Jennings is our host. We must show her some attention.

(*Pause.* **MARIANNE** *continues to look out of the window.*)

I saw Mr. Willoughby's card on the table in the hall. Were you in when he called?

MARIANNE. No. More's the pity.

(*Pause.*)

ELINOR. You have no confidence in me, Marianne.

MARIANNE. (*Turning from the window.*) This reproach from you, Elinor – you who have confidence in no one!

ELINOR. Me! Indeed, Marianne, I have nothing to tell.

MARIANNE. Nor I. Our situations then are alike. We have neither of us anything to tell; you, because you do not communicate, and I, because I conceal nothing.

(*Pause. Knocking at the door.*)

Oh Elinor, it is Willoughby, indeed it is!

(*She heads for the door and almost rushes directly into the arms of* **COLONEL BRANDON**, *who enters to her.*)

(**ELINOR** *rises to greet him, and* **MARIANNE** *retreats, disappointed and embarrassed.*)

(*Exit* **MARIANNE**.)

(**ELINOR** *does her best to recover her spirits and distract from her sister's rudeness.*)

ELINOR. Colonel Brandon. We had not expected to see you so soon.

BRANDON. I hope I am not intruding. Is your sister unwell?

ELINOR. She has been in low spirits.

BRANDON. Indeed, I am troubled to hear it. I hope she soon recovers her health.

ELINOR. You are very kind.

BRANDON. I am charged by Sir John to request your presence at a ball this Friday. He earnestly hopes that the Miss Dashwoods might join the company.

ELINOR. I am sure we should be delighted.

BRANDON. Thank you. I will convey your answer with pleasure.

(**BRANDON** *bows;* **ELINOR** *curtseys;* **BRANDON** *exits.*)

ELINOR. I only pray we may see Mr. Willoughby there.

(*Exit* **ELINOR**.)

Scene Two

(*Enter* SIR JOHN, LUCY, MRS. JENNINGS, BRANDON, MARIANNE, *and* ELINOR, *who all take their places as at a ball.*)

[MUSIC CUE "MRS. JENNINGS' DANCE"]

[*Note: If extra time is required for a costume change for the Dashwood sisters, enter* SIR JOHN *and* MRS. JENNINGS, *who dance, to the tune of "Mrs. Jennings' Dance"; then enter* LUCY, BRANDON, MARIANNE, *and* ELINOR.]

[MUSIC CUE "UPON A SUMMER'S DAY"]

(*They dance:* BRANDON *with* ELINOR, *and* SIR JOHN *with* LUCY, *while* MRS. JENNINGS *sits, cheerful, on the sidelines, and* MARIANNE *sits, uninterested, next to her.*)

(*The music ceases, and* MRS. JENNINGS *approachs* BRANDON *and* ELINOR.)

MRS. JENNINGS. Well, Colonel, I have brought several young ladies with me, you see – that is, you see but one of them now, but there is another somewhere, and your friend Miss Marianne, too – which you will not be sorry to hear. I do not know what you and Mr. Willoughby will do between you about her. Aye, it is a fine thing to be young and handsome. Well! I was young once, but I was never handsome – worse luck for me. However, I got a very good husband, and I don't know what the greatest beauty can do more. Ah! Poor man! He has been dead these eight years and better. But here I am rambling on, and you'll want to talk to your fair partner, Colonel! Then see if you can't get Marianne to hop about a bit. I hate to see a pretty girl sitting down at a ball.

(MRS. JENNINGS *joins* LUCY.)

(*Enter* JOHN DASHWOOD.)

(While **ELINOR** *and* **BRANDON** *speak,* **MRS. JENNINGS** *accosts* **JOHN** *and introduces* **LUCY**.*)*

BRANDON. Tell me, Miss Dashwood, when am I to congratulate you on the acquisition of a brother?

ELINOR. A brother, Colonel? Whatever can you mean?

BRANDON. Your sister's engagement to Mr. Willoughby is very generally known.

ELINOR. It cannot be generally known, for her own family does not know it.

BRANDON. I beg your pardon, I am afraid my inquiry has been impertinent; but I had not supposed any secrecy intended, as their marriage is universally talked of.

ELINOR. How can that be? By whom can you have heard it mentioned?

BRANDON. By many – by Mrs. Jennings, and Miss Steele, among others. But still I might not have believed it if I had not, when the servant let me in today, accidentally seen a letter, directed to Mr. Willoughby in your sister's writing. Is every thing finally settled? Is it impossible to...? But I have no right, and I could have no chance of succeeding. Tell me that it is all absolutely resolved on.

ELINOR. I can only tell you that you seem to know much more of the matter than I. But perhaps Mr. Willoughby will resolve us tonight? I understand he was invited.

BRANDON. Indeed. Well, to your sister I wish all imaginable happiness; to Willoughby that he may endeavour to deserve her.

*(***BRANDON*** exits.)*

*(***JOHN*** approaches ***ELINOR***.)*

JOHN. My dear Elinor! I wished very much to call upon you yesterday, but we have been taken up with Fanny's brother, Robert. He has been staying with some friends in the country, at Lady Eliott's seat, and there has been much to-do to get him settled, for Robert can never bear to fall behind with the London fashions. And then this morning I had fully intended to call on you, if I could possibly find a spare half-hour, but one has always so much to do on first coming to town. Tomorrow we shall certainly be able to call upon you and your friend Mrs. Jennings, in Berkeley Street. Mrs. Jennings seems to be a woman of good fortune.

ELINOR. I believe so.

JOHN. She and Sir John are excellent neighbours to you in the country, I understand.

ELINOR. Excellent indeed. Their attention to our comfort, their friendliness in every particular, is more than I can express.

JOHN. I am extremely glad to hear it, upon my word; extremely glad indeed. But so it ought to be; they are people of large fortune, they are related to you, and every civility and accommodation that can serve to make your situation pleasant might be reasonably expected. And so you are most comfortably settled in your little cottage and want for nothing! It was a great satisfaction to us to hear it, I assure you.

> (*Enter* **WILLOUGHBY**, *by the other door. He sees* **ELINOR** *and* **MARIANNE** *but does not acknowledge them – he instead enters into conversation with* **SIR JOHN**.)

> (**MARIANNE** *sees him.*)

MARIANNE. Willoughby!

> (*He turns, looking a little discomposed, but withdraws slightly as she approaches him.*)

Good God! Willoughby, what is the meaning of this? Have you not received my letters? Will you not shake hands with me?

WILLOUGHBY. Yes, of course. I did myself the honour of calling in Berkeley Street last Tuesday, and very much regretted that I was not fortunate enough to find yourselves and Mrs. Jennings at home.

MARIANNE. But have you not received my notes? Tell me, Willoughby, for heaven's sake tell me, what is the matter?

WILLOUGHBY. Yes, I had the pleasure of receiving the information of your arrival in town, which you were so good as to send me.

MARIANNE. Good God Willoughby! What does this mean?

WILLOUGHBY. Nothing. Good evening, madam.

> *(Exit* **WILLOUGHBY.** **MARIANNE** *stumbles to* **ELINOR***, who hurries forward to join her, as* **JOHN** *draws back, disapproving.)*

MARIANNE. Go to him, Elinor, and force him to come to me. Tell him I must see him again – must speak to him instantly. I cannot rest – I shall not have a moment's peace till this is explained. Oh, go to him, this moment.

ELINOR. How can that be done? No, my dearest Marianne, you must wait. This is not the place for explanations.

> *(***MARIANNE** *nearly faints.* **ELINOR** *supports her.)*

Mrs. Jennings? I'm afraid we must return home. My sister is unwell.

[MUSIC CUE "BLACK-EY'D SUSAN"]

> *(All crowd around* **MARIANNE** *with concern or curiosity, and exit.)*

Scene Three

(We are at Mrs. Jennings' residence in London.)

(Enter **MRS. JENNINGS**, *accompanied by* **ELINOR**.*)*

MRS. JENNINGS. Upon my word, I never saw a young woman so desperately in love in my life! *My* girls were nothing to her, and yet they used to be foolish enough; but as for Miss Marianne, she is quite an altered creature. I hope, from the bottom of my heart, he won't keep her waiting much longer, for it is quite grievous to see her look so ill and forlorn. Pray, when are they to be married?

ELINOR. And have you really, ma'am, talked yourself into a persuasion of my sister's being engaged to Mr. Willoughby? I thought it had been only a joke, but so serious a question seems to imply more; and I must beg, therefore, that you will not deceive yourself any longer.

MRS. JENNINGS. For shame, for shame, Miss Dashwood! How can you talk so? Don't we all know that it must be a match, that they were over head and ears in love with each other from the first moment they met? Did not I see them together in Devonshire every day, and all day long? Come, come, this won't do. Because you are so sly about it yourself, you think nobody else has any senses; but I can tell you, it has been known all over town this ever so long. I tell everybody of it.

ELINOR. Indeed, ma'am, you are mistaken. Indeed, you are doing a very unkind thing in spreading the report.

MRS. JENNINGS. Well, we will see what the morning brings.

(Exit **MRS. JENNINGS** *with* **ELINOR**.*)*

Scene Four

[MUSIC CUE "WILLOUGHBY'S LETTER"]

(Enter **MARIANNE**, *a letter in her hands. Enter* **WILLOUGHBY**, *above. As* **MARIANNE** *reads the letter,* **WILLOUGHBY** *speaks its contents to the audience.)*

WILLOUGHBY. My dear madam, I am much concerned to find there was anything in my behaviour last night that did not meet your approbation; and though I am quite at a loss to discover in what point I could be so unfortunate as to offend you, I entreat your forgiveness of what I can assure you to have been perfectly unintentional. I shall never reflect on my former acquaintance with your family in Devonshire without the most grateful pleasure, and flatter myself it will not be broken by any mistake or misapprehension of my actions. My esteem for your whole family is very sincere; but if I have been so unfortunate as to give rise to a belief of more than I felt, or meant to express, I shall reproach myself for not having been more guarded in my professions of that esteem. That I should ever have meant more you will allow to be impossible, when you understand that my affections have been long engaged elsewhere, and it will not be many weeks, I believe, before this engagement is fulfilled. It is with great regret, therefore, that I return your letters, and the lock of hair, which you so obligingly bestowed on me.

*(***MARIANNE** *crumples to the floor. Exit* **WILLOUGHBY**.*)*

(The music ceases as **ELINOR** *runs in.)*

ELINOR. Oh my poor Marianne! I only wish there were anything I could do which might be of comfort to you.

MARIANNE. O Elinor, I have never been so miserable!

ELINOR. Exert yourself, dear Marianne, if you would not kill yourself and all who love you. Think of your mother;

think of her misery while *you* suffer: for her sake you must exert yourself.

MARIANNE. I cannot, I cannot, leave me, leave me, if I distress you; leave me, hate me, forget me! But do not torture me so. Oh! How easy for those who have no sorrow of their own to talk of exertion! Happy, happy Elinor, *you* cannot have an idea of what I suffer.

ELINOR. Do you call *me* happy, Marianne? Ah! If you knew! – And can you believe me to be so, while I see you so wretched?

MARIANNE. *(Throwing her arms round her sister.)* Forgive me, forgive me! I know you feel for me; I know what a heart you have; but yet you are – you must be – happy; Edward loves you – what, oh what, can do away such happiness as that?

ELINOR. Many, many circumstances.

MARIANNE. No, no, no, he loves you, and only you. You can have no grief.

ELINOR. I can have no pleasure while I see you in this state.

MARIANNE. And you will never see me otherwise. Mine is a misery which nothing can do away.

ELINOR. You must not talk so, Marianne. Have you no comforts? No friends? Is your loss such as leaves no opening for consolation? Much as you suffer now, think of what you would have suffered if the discovery of his character had been delayed to a later period – if your engagement had been carried on for months and months...

MARIANNE. Engagement! There has been no engagement.

ELINOR. No engagement!

MARIANNE. No, he is not so unworthy as you believe him. He has broken no faith with me.

ELINOR. But he told you that he loved you.

MARIANNE. Yes – no – never absolutely. It was every day implied, but never professedly declared. Sometimes I thought it had been – but it never was. I felt myself to be as solemnly engaged to him, as if the strictest legal covenant had bound us to each other.

ELINOR. I can believe it, but unfortunately he did not feel the same.

MARIANNE. He *did* feel the same, Elinor – for weeks and weeks he felt it. I know he did. Have you forgot the morning that we parted? When he told me that it might be many weeks before we met again – his distress – can I ever forget his distress?

(Taking up the letter.) It is too much! Oh, Willoughby, Willoughby, could this be yours? Cruel, cruel – nothing can acquit you. Willoughby, where was your heart when you wrote those words?

(Enter **MRS. JENNINGS**.*)*

MRS. JENNINGS. Oh! And how do you do, my dears?

*(**MARIANNE** turns away, sobbing.)*

How is she, Miss Dashwood? Poor thing! She looks very bad. No wonder. I heard but half an hour ago that Willoughby is to be married very soon, to a Miss Grey. A good-for-nothing fellow, I have no patience with him. It is the oddest thing to me, that a man should use such a pretty girl so ill! But when there is plenty of money on one side, and next to none on the other…

*(**ELINOR** embraces her sister, who continues to weep.)*

ELINOR. Then this Miss Grey is rich?

MRS. JENNINGS. Fifty thousand pounds, my dear. Did you ever see her? A smart, stylish girl, they say, but not handsome. Fifty thousand pounds! And by all accounts it won't come before it's wanted, with his dashing about with his curricle and his hunters! When a young man comes and makes love to a pretty girl, he has no business to fly off only because he grows poor, and a richer girl is ready to have him. Why don't he, in such a case, sell his horses, let his house, turn off his servants, and make a thorough reform at once? But that won't do nowadays – nothing in the way of pleasure can ever be given up by the young men of this age. Poor dear – can I do anything for her? I have just recollected that I have some of the finest old Constantia wine in the house that was ever tasted – my poor late husband! How fond he was of it! Whenever he had a touch of his old cholicky gout, he said it did him more good than anything else in the world – perhaps it may help your sister?

ELINOR. Dear ma'am, this kindness is quite unnecessary. I believe nothing will do her so much good as rest.

MRS. JENNINGS. Well, I will leave you to venture out, my dear, and I will see if we can't find something to tempt her with. There's a shop with the sweetest dried cherries – perhaps they may comfort her.

ELINOR. You are very kind.

(Exit **MRS. JENNINGS.***)*

You must go and rest, my love. You cannot have slept at all.

MARIANNE. I cannot rest, Elinor.

ELINOR. You must –

(Enter **LUCY.***)*

LUCY. If I might disturb you –

(Exit **MARIANNE**, *at speed.)*

Oh, I am so sorry that your sister is unwell, Miss Dashwood.

ELINOR. You are very good. My sister will be sorry to miss the pleasure of seeing you, but she has been very much plagued lately with nervous headaches, which make her unfit for conversation.

LUCY. Oh, dear me, that is a great pity! But it is well that we can be alone. My dear friend! I come to you to talk of happiness.

(She hurries forward to take **ELINOR**'s *hand, and leads her to sit beside her.)*

You know I spoke to your charming brother at the ball. Well, dear John was sweet enough to invite me to call on Fanny, and I took the liberty of doing so this morning.

ELINOR. Indeed?

LUCY. And who should be there, but Mrs. Ferrars, Edward's mother! You know how I had dreaded the thought of seeing her, but the very moment I was introduced, there was such an affability in her behaviour, as seemed to say, she had taken a fancy to me. Nothing could be more flattering than her way of treating me! So exceedingly affable! Are you not pleased for me, Elinor? Does this not bode well for my future happiness?

ELINOR. Undoubtedly, if she had known your engagement, nothing could be more flattering than this treatment of you; but as that was not the case –

LUCY. I guessed you would say so, but there is no reason in the world why she should seem to like me, if she did not – and her liking me is everything. You shan't talk me out of my satisfaction. Mrs. Ferrars is a charming woman, and so is your sister-in-law. I wonder that I never heard you say how agreeable dear Fanny is!

> *(Pause.)*

Are you ill, Miss Dashwood? You seem low.

ELINOR. I never was in better health.

LUCY. I am glad of it with all my heart, but really you do not look it. I should be so sorry to have *you* ill – you, that have been the greatest comfort in the world. Indeed, I am perfectly convinced of your regard for me, and next to Edward's love, it is the greatest comfort I have.

> *(Knocking at the door.)*
>
> *(Enter **MARIANNE**, at speed.)*

MARIANNE. Who is at the door?

> *(Ignorning **LUCY**, she runs to the window.)*

ELINOR. Marianne –

MARIANNE. It is Edward! Dearest Edward!

> (*She turns to look at* **ELINOR**, *who looks to* **LUCY**. *Moments of frozen suspense, and then:*)
>
> (*Enter* **EDWARD**.)
>
> (**MARIANNE** *hurries to greet him.*)

Dear Edward! This a moment of great happiness! This would almost make amends for everything.

EDWARD. (*Taking her hand.*) Marianne –

> (**EDWARD** *turns to look for* **ELINOR** *and sees* **LUCY**. *He freezes, still holding* **MARIANNE**'s *hand.*)

ELINOR. (*Flustered.*) Edward.

LUCY. (*Murmured.*) Mr. Ferrars.

> (**ELINOR** *and* **LUCY** *curtsey, and* **EDWARD** *gives an awkward bow.*)

ELINOR. Won't you sit down?

> (*They sit,* **MARIANNE** *looking with speaking tenderness toward* **EDWARD** *and* **ELINOR**, **ELINOR** *steadfastly avoiding her gaze,* **LUCY** *narrowly watching* **ELINOR**, *and* **EDWARD** *doing his best to look at nothing at all.*)

I hope you are well.

EDWARD. I am.

> (*Pause.*)

Thank you.

> (*Pause.*)

ELINOR. I imagine you know that we are come to London with Mrs. Jennings, for a few weeks.

EDWARD. Ah.

ELINOR. Our mother remains at Barton.

EDWARD. I see.

> (*Pause.*)

And your mother – you left your mother well?

ELINOR. Yes. Thank you.

> *(Pause.)*

EDWARD. And Miss Steele? You are well also?

LUCY. *(With emphasis.)* I am well *now*, Mr. Ferrars.

> *(Pause.)*

EDWARD. *(Rousing himself.)* I am sorry to hear you're unwell, Marianne. I fear London does not agree with you.

MARIANNE. Oh, don't think of me! Don't think of *my* health. Elinor is well, you see. That must be enough for us both.

> *(Pause.)*

EDWARD. Do you like London?

MARIANNE. Not at all. I expected much pleasure in it, but I have found none. The sight of you, Edward, is the only comfort it has afforded; and, thank heaven, you are what you always were!

> *(Pause.)*

I think, Elinor, we must employ Edward to take care of us in our return to Barton. In a week or two, I suppose, we shall be going; and, I trust, Edward will not be very unwilling to accept the charge.

> **(EDWARD** *mutters something inaudible.)*

But why have you not come to see us yet?

EDWARD. I have been engaged elsewhere.

MARIANNE. Engaged! But what was that, when such friends were to be met?

LUCY. Perhaps, Miss Marianne, you think young men never stand upon engagements, if they have no mind to keep them, little as well as great.

> **(ELINOR** *flinches, but* **MARIANNE** *remains calm.)*

MARIANNE. No, indeed. I am sure Edward's engagements were most pressing and necessary, for he is the most fearful of giving pain, of wounding expectation, and the most incapable of being selfish of anybody I ever saw.

(**EDWARD** *coughs and looks uncomfortable.*)

Edward, it is so and I will say it. What – are you never to hear yourself praised? Any friend of mine must submit to my open commendation, and you are particularly deserving of it – is he not, Elinor?

ELINOR. *(Softly.)* Indeed.

LUCY. Edward certainly has the sweetest character *I* have ever encountered.

(Pause.)

EDWARD. *(Rising.)* Forgive me, but I must take my leave.

(They all rise.)

MARIANNE. Going so soon! My dear Edward, this must not be.

EDWARD. I fear I must.

LUCY. Do you go to your mother's?

EDWARD. Well, I –

LUCY. Then perhaps you would be so good as to accompany me on my errands, Mr. Ferrars?

(She takes his arm.)

I have promised to meet dear Mrs. Jennings, and the shop lies on your way.

EDWARD. Certainly, I – certainly. Good day, Elinor; Marianne.

ELINOR. Good day, Edward.

MARIANNE. We shall hope to see you soon, Edward!

*(Exit **EDWARD** and **LUCY**.)*

Why did she not leave on her errands sooner? Could she not see that we wanted her gone? How teasing to Edward!

ELINOR. Why so? We are all his friends, and Lucy has been as long known to him as any. It is but natural he should like to see her as well as ourselves.

MARIANNE. You know, Elinor, this is the kind of talking I cannot bear.

(Knocking at the door.)

ELINOR. Who can this be now? I thought we had been safe.

MARIANNE. *(Looking out of the window.)* It is Colonel Brandon. We are never safe from *him*.

(Exit **MARIANNE.***)*

(Enter **COLONEL BRANDON,** *by the other door.)*

BRANDON. Miss Dashwood.

ELINOR. Colonel Brandon!

BRANDON. Please forgive the intrusion. I met Mrs. Jennings in the street, and she encouraged me to come on; and I was the more easily encouraged, because I thought it probable that I might find you alone. My object – my wish – is to be a means of giving comfort – no, I must not say comfort – but conviction, lasting conviction to your sister's mind. My regard for her – will you allow me to prove it, by relating some circumstances which nothing but a very sincere regard – nothing but an earnest desire of being useful – I think I am justified...

(Pause.)

ELINOR. I understand you. You have something to tell me of Mr. Willoughby, that will open his character further. Your telling it will be the greatest act of friendship that can be shown Marianne. Pray, pray let me hear it.

BRANDON. You have probably entirely forgotten a conversation between us one evening at Barton Park in which I alluded to a lady I had once known, as resembling your sister Marianne.

ELINOR. Indeed, I have *not* forgotten it.

BRANDON. There is a very strong resemblance between them: the same warmth of heart, the same eagerness of fancy and spirits. This lady was an orphan from her infancy, and under the guardianship of my father. Our ages were nearly the same, and from our earliest years we were playfellows and friends. I cannot remember the time when I did not love Eliza; and my affection for her was such as perhaps, judging from my present forlorn and cheerless gravity, you might think me incapable of having ever felt. At seventeen she was lost to me forever. She was married against her inclination to my brother. My brother did not deserve her; he did not even love her. We were within a few hours of eloping together for Scotland. The treachery, or folly, of her maid betrayed us. The blow was a severe one. My brother had no regard for her; his pleasures were not what they ought to have been, and from the first he treated her unkindly. The consequence of this, upon a mind so young, so lively, so inexperienced as Eliza's, was but too natural. Can we wonder that, with such a husband to provoke inconstancy, she should fall? The shock which her marriage had given me, was of trifling weight – was nothing to what I felt when I heard, about two years afterwards, of her divorce...

(He stops and paces silently for a while, collecting his thoughts.)

ELINOR. Go on.

(Unseen by them both, enter **MARIANNE**, *who listens.)*

BRANDON. When I received the news, I was with my regiment in the East Indies. It was nearly three years after this unhappy period before I returned to England. My first care, when I *did* arrive, was of course to seek for her; but the search was as fruitless as it was melancholy. I could not trace her beyond her first seducer, and there was every reason to fear that she had removed from him only to sink deeper in a life of sin. At last, however, and after I had been six months in England, I *did* find her. So altered, worn down by acute suffering of every kind! I saw her placed in comfortable lodgings; I visited her every day during the rest of her short life; I was with her in her last moments... She left to my care her only child, named Eliza after her mother, the offspring of her first guilty connection. I had no family, no home; and my little Eliza was therefore placed at school. Last February, just before her sixteenth birthday, she suddenly disappeared. I could learn nothing of her whereabouts for months. What I thought, what I feared, may be imagined.

ELINOR. Good heavens! Could it be – could Willoughby!

(**MARIANNE** *near-swoons and steadies herself against the wall.*)

BRANDON. The first news that reached me of her came in a letter from herself; I received it on the very morning of our intended party to Whitwell, and this was the reason of my leaving Barton so suddenly. Little did Mr. Willoughby imagine, I suppose, when his looks censured me for incivility in breaking up the party, that I was called away to the relief of one whom he had made poor and miserable; but *had* he known it, would he have been less gay or less happy in the smiles of your sister? No, he had already done that, which no man who *can* feel for another would do. He had left the girl whose youth and innocence he had seduced, with no home, no help, no friends, ignorant of his address! She was in a situation of the utmost distress, for she was with child – his child. Knowing this, he had left her, promising to return; he neither returned, nor wrote, nor relieved her.

ELINOR. This is beyond everything!

BRANDON. Indeed.

ELINOR. Have you ever seen Mr. Willoughby since you left him at Barton?

BRANDON. Yes, once I have. One meeting was unavoidable...

[MUSIC CUE "WILLOUGHBY'S THEME"]

(*Enter* **WILLOUGHBY**, *below. Both are armed with swords.*)

(*They duel while* **ELINOR** *watches.*)

(**BRANDON** *vanquishes* **WILLOUGHBY** *without drawing blood, successfully disarming him, and holds his sword to* **WILLOUGHBY**'s *throat. A pause, and then he steps back, granting* **WILLOUGHBY** *his life.*)

(*Exit* **WILLOUGHBY**, *at a run.* **BRANDON** *sheaths his sword and returns to* **ELINOR**.)

BRANDON. His character is now before you. Knowing all this, as I have now known it many weeks, only guess what I must have felt on seeing your sister as fond of him as ever, and on being assured that she was to marry him: guess what I must have felt for all your sakes.

ELINOR. Thank you, Colonel Brandon, for telling me this. Though it will pain Marianne to hear it, I know that, in time, it will help her recover. You have done a great service to us both.

(**BRANDON** *bows and exits.*)

(**ELINOR** *sits, shaken by what she has heard.*)

(**MARIANNE** *approaches her.*)

MARIANNE. Oh, Elinor...

ELINOR. Dearest – you could not have known – we could not have known –

MARIANNE. Elinor, how could he? How *could* he? And how could I be so deceived in him?

(*A pause while they embrace. Then* **ELINOR** *gently leads her sister off.*)

Scene Five

[MUSIC CUE "LONDON THEME"]

(Time passes. Enter **ELINOR** *with needlework.)*

(Enter **MARIANNE**, *a little neater than before, but still visibly ill. She paces back and forth, sometimes reading Willoughby's letter, sometimes simply pacing.)*

ELINOR. Dear Marianne, will you not come and sit with me?

MARIANNE. No, Elinor. Do not ask me to sit still.

ELINOR. We could sew, or perhaps read aloud. If you could only distract yourself –

MARIANNE. I cannot. Do not ask it.

(Pause.)

(Enter **MRS. JENNINGS** *and* **JOHN DASHWOOD**.)

MRS. JENNINGS. My dears, my dears, your brother has come to see you – and with such news – such news!

JOHN. Sisters, you must prepare yourselves. I have terrible news. Poor Fanny is beside herself. Her brother, Edward, has been discovered to be engaged to Miss Lucy Steele! It seems they have kept it a most illicit secret for a number of years, until Miss Steele, who was visiting our family, actually announced it to Mrs. Ferrars – I believe she expected his mother to be pleased – pleased! – at such an alliance. Mrs. Ferrars has suffered dreadfully – it has been a scene of such complicated distress – but I will hope that the storm may be weathered without any of us being quite overcome. Poor Fanny! She has borne it all with the fortitude of an angel. Of course, Mrs. Ferrars sent for Edward, but all that Mrs. Ferrars could say to make him put an end to the engagement, assisted too by my arguments and Fanny's entreaties, was of no avail. Duty, affection, everything was disregarded. I never thought Edward so stubborn, so unfeeling before.

MARIANNE. Gracious God! Can this be possible?

JOHN. Well may you wonder, Marianne, at his obstinacy. Edward said very little; but what he did say, was in the most determined manner. Nothing should prevail on him to give up his engagement. He would stand to it, cost him what it might.

MRS. JENNINGS. Then he has acted like an honest man! I beg your pardon, Mr. Dashwood, but if he had done otherwise, I should have thought him a rascal.

JOHN. Indeed, ma'am. Edward's brother, Robert, has spent all day with the girl, trying to convince her to release Edward from the engagement, but she will not budge. I am sorry to say that Edward is dismissed forever from his mother's notice. He left her house yesterday, but where he is gone, or whether he is still in town, I do not know; for *we* of course can make no inquiry.

MRS. JENNINGS. Poor young man! What is to become of him?

JOHN. It is a melancholy consideration. Born to the prospect of such affluence! I cannot conceive a situation more deplorable. But as it is, it must be out of anybody's power to assist him. His mother has determined, with a very natural kind of spirit, to settle *that* estate upon Robert immediately, which might have been Edward's. I left her this morning with her lawyer, talking over the business.

MRS. JENNINGS. Well! That is *her* revenge. Everybody has a way of their own. But I don't think mine would be, to make one son rich, because another had plagued me.

JOHN. I am sure I appreciate the sentiment, ma'am, but I cannot share in it. In any case, it is a shocking business, and I thought you ought to know of it at once.

ELINOR. Yes. Thank you.

JOHN. And now, I take my leave. When do you return to Devonshire?

ELINOR. As soon as possible. My sister's health makes it necessary, and Mrs. Jennings has kindly offered to convey us.

JOHN. Then I shall give your regards to Fanny. Good day to you all.

*(Exit **JOHN**.)*

MRS. JENNINGS. What a to-do, my dears! I must go and see poor Lucy, at once!

*(Exit **MRS. JENNINGS**.)*

MARIANNE. God, Elinor, can it be true? But I thought – I knew – we all did... How long has this been known to you?

ELINOR. On our arrival in London, Lucy told me of her engagement, in the strictest confidence.

MARIANNE. These few weeks! So calm! – So cheerful! – How have you been supported?

ELINOR. *(Turning away.)* By feeling that I was doing my duty. My promise to Lucy obliged me to be secret. I have very often wished to undeceive yourself and my mother, but without betraying her trust, I never could have convinced you.

MARIANNE. Weeks! – And yet you loved him!

ELINOR. Yes. But I did not love only him; and while the comfort of others was dear to me, I was glad to spare them from knowing how much I felt. Edward must do his duty, and though he may harbour some regret, in the end, I wish he may be happy. Edward will marry Lucy; and time and habit will teach him to forget that he ever thought another superior to *her*.

MARIANNE. If such is your way of thinking, if the loss of what is most valued is so easily to be made up by something else, your self-command is perhaps a little less to be wondered at.

ELINOR. I understand you. You do not suppose that I have ever felt much. For weeks, Marianne, I have had all this hanging on my mind, without being at liberty to speak of it to a single creature. I have known myself to be divided from Edward forever. Nothing has proved him unworthy; nor has anything declared him indifferent

to me. If you can think me capable of ever feeling –
surely you may suppose that I have suffered *now*. The
composure of mind has been the effect of constant and
painful exertion. I have been *very* unhappy.

MARIANNE. *(Much affected.)* Oh! Elinor, you have made
me hate myself forever. How barbarous have I been to
you! – You, who have been my only comfort, who have
borne with me in all my misery, who have seemed to be
only suffering for me! All we can hope for is to return
soon to Mama. Come, let us make ready.

(Exit **MARIANNE** *and* **ELINOR***, arm in arm.)*

ACT V

Scene One

(The hills near Barton.)

*(**MARIANNE** enters, wandering alone through a storm. Storm sound effects.)*

MARIANNE. Here is Barton Valley. Look up to it, Marianne, and be tranquil if you can. Look at those hills! Did you ever see their equals? To the left is Barton Park, amongst those exalted trees. And there, beneath that farthest hill, which rises with such grandeur, is our cottage, where so much has passed – and below, in that winding valley, is Allenham, which I once hoped should be mine. Oh Willoughby – whatever may have changed you now, I was once as dear to you as my own soul could wish. Have you forgot the moment we parted, when you told me that it might be many weeks before we met again? Your distress – can I ever forget your distress?

> *(She stumbles and collapses in a shivering heap.)*

Willoughby...

> *(**MARIANNE** lies alone center stage. There is a pause of such length that it seems she may die there, alone.)*

> *(Enter **ELINOR**.)*

ELINOR. Marianne! What has happened? Oh, good God! Help! Somebody help! My sister has collapsed. *(Trying to wake **MARIANNE**.)* Help, somebody!

(There is another desperate pause, and then
BRANDON *enters, assesses the situation*
instantly, and carries **MARIANNE** *away,*
assisted by **ELINOR**, *who hurries after him.)*

**[MUSIC CUE "BLACK-EY'D SUSAN -
STORM TRANSITION"]**

Scene Two

(We are in the parlour of Barton Cottage.)

(Enter **MRS. JENNINGS** *and* **MRS. DASHWOOD**.*)*

MRS. DASHWOOD. She is not as well as we could wish, Mrs. Jennings. The doctor looked grave when he went in earlier, and poor Elinor has been nursing her all night. We've none of us slept in two days.

MRS. JENNINGS. And Colonel Brandon has been here the whole time. What a man! He carried her here as if she weighed no more than a feather. Poor, dear Marianne. She has never been the same since that cruel man jilted her. If the Colonel had not arrived, I do not know what might have happened!

MRS. DASHWOOD. Pray don't conjecture! Are the circumstances not bad enough already? Dear Lord, my poor daughter.

(Enter **ELINOR**.*)*

MRS. JENNINGS. What news, my dear?

MRS. DASHWOOD. She is not worse, I hope?

ELINOR. Not worse, indeed, ma'am, no. She may be a little better. Colonel Brandon and the doctor are still with her, but she is sleeping now, and I think you may go up to see her without any danger.

MRS. DASHWOOD. Thank you, my dear.

(She exits in the direction of Marianne's bedroom, followed by **MRS. JENNINGS**.*)*

*(***ELINOR** *begins, very softly, to cry.)*

(Enter **WILLOUGHBY**, *for once uncertain.)*

*(***ELINOR** *moves to leave the room.)*

WILLOUGHBY. Miss Dashwood, for half an hour – for ten minutes – I entreat you to stay.

ELINOR. No, sir, I shall *not* stay. Your business cannot be with *me*.

WILLOUGHBY. On the contrary, my business is with you, and only you.

ELINOR. With me! Well, sir, be quick. I have no time to spare.

WILLOUGHBY. Your sister is out of danger. I heard it from the servant. God be praised! But is it true? Is it really true?

(**ELINOR** *is deliberately and coldly silent.*)

For God's sake tell me, is she out of danger, or is she not?

ELINOR. We hope she is.

(*Pause.*)

WILLOUGHBY. Tell me honestly, Miss Dashwood: do you think me most a knave or a fool?

ELINOR. Mr. Willoughby, you *ought* to feel, and I certainly *do*, that after what has passed your coming here in this manner, and forcing yourself upon my notice, requires a very particular excuse. What is it that you mean by it?

WILLOUGHBY. I mean, if I can, to make you hate me one degree less than you do *now*. I mean to offer some kind of explanation, some kind of apology, for the past; to open my whole heart to you, and by convincing you, that though I have been always a blockhead, I have not been always a rascal, to obtain something like forgiveness from Ma–...from your sister.

ELINOR. Is this the real reason of your coming?

WILLOUGHBY. Upon my soul it is. When I first became intimate with your family, I had no other intention than to pass my time pleasantly while I was obliged to remain in Devonshire, more pleasantly than I had ever done before. Your sister's lovely person and interesting manners could not but please me; and her behaviour to me almost from the first was so charming... But at first, I must confess, my vanity only was elevated by it. Careless of her happiness, thinking only of my own amusement, giving way to feelings which I had always been too much in the habit of indulging, I endeavoured, by every means in my power, to make myself pleasing to her, without any design of returning her affection.

ELINOR. It is hardly worthwhile, Mr. Willoughby, for you to relate, or for me to listen any longer. Such a beginning as this cannot be followed by anything.

WILLOUGHBY. I insist on your hearing the whole of it. It had been for some time my intention to marry a woman of fortune. To attach myself to your sister, therefore, was not a thing to be thought of. But one thing may be said for me: even in that horrid state of selfish vanity, I did not know the extent of the injury I meditated, because I did not *then* know what it was to love. My relations with Marianne changed all that.

ELINOR. You did then believe yourself at one time attached to my sister?

WILLOUGHBY. To have resisted such attractions, to have withstood such tenderness! – Is there a man on earth who could have done it? The happiest hours of my life were those I spent with her when I felt my intentions were strictly honourable, and my feelings blameless. Had not fate intervened, you must believe that I truly intended to marry her.

ELINOR. What happened?

WILLOUGHBY. I imagine you have heard something of my past? From Colonel Brandon, no doubt...

ELINOR. I have, I have heard it all. And how you will explain away any part of your guilt in that dreadful business, I confess is beyond my comprehension.

WILLOUGHBY. I will not attempt to deny my guilt. But before I could propose to Marianne, it was this past history of mine – my relations with Eliza – that came to light, and I was disinherited. That left me with nothing, and I immediately determined that my only way out of poverty was to marry a rich woman, as I had originally intended. My affection for Marianne, my thorough conviction of her attachment to me...it was all insufficient to outweigh that dread of poverty. Oh, God! What a hard-hearted rascal I was!

ELINOR. So you resolved to marry Miss Grey – now Mrs. Willoughby?

WILLOUGHBY. God forgive me, yes.

ELINOR. That is a hard-hearted way to discuss your wife.

WILLOUGHBY. Of course; I am sorry. I never meant to see your sister again. Well, at last, as I need not tell you, Marianne and I did meet; and what an evening of agony it was! Marianne, beautiful as an angel, calling me Willoughby in such a tone! Holding out her hand to me, asking me for an explanation, with those bewitching eyes fixed in such speaking solicitude on my face! – Oh, God!

(Pause.)

Well, let me make haste and be gone. Your sister is certainly better, certainly out of danger?

ELINOR. We believe so.

(**WILLOUGHBY** *turns to go.*)

But the letter, Mr. Willoughby, your own letter to my sister, which made her so wretched; have you anything to say about that?

WILLOUGHBY. Yes, yes, *that* in particular. Your sister wrote to me the next morning after I abandoned her that night, and her letter happened to catch my wife's eye before it caught mine. Some vague report had reached her before of my attachment to a young lady in Devonshire, and she was somewhat jealous. Affecting that air of playfulness, therefore, which is delightful in a woman one loves, she opened the letter directly, and read its contents. She was well paid for her impudence. She read what made her wretched. Her wretchedness I could have borne, but her passion...her malice...in short: what do you think of my wife's style of letter-writing?

ELINOR. Your wife! The letter was in your own handwriting.

WILLOUGHBY. But she dictated every syllable.

ELINOR. Yet that does not excuse you from the blame of sending it.

>   *(Pause.)*

Despite that, you have proved yourself less faulty than I had believed you. You have proved your heart less wicked. But I hardly know – the misery that you have inflicted – I hardly know what could have made it worse.

WILLOUGHBY. I understand. But what I felt on hearing that your sister was dying – and dying too, believing me the greatest villain upon earth, scorning, hating me in her last moments! I had to come. And now that I have told you all, I take my leave.

>   *(**WILLOUGHBY** extends his hand. After a moment, **ELINOR** takes it.)*

Please remember me to your sister. Goodbye. God bless you!

>   *(Exit **WILLOUGHBY**, almost running from the room.)*

ELINOR. And may that be the last we ever see of Willoughby.

>   *(Exit **ELINOR**, slow and thoughtful, by the other door.)*

Scene Three

[MUSIC CUE "THE JOYS OF THE COUNTRY"]

(Time passes. We are outside Barton Cottage.)

*(**COLONEL BRANDON** visits with a basket, knocking at the cottage door; is received with great friendliness by **MRS. DASHWOOD**; and then departs again.)*

*(**ELINOR** steps outside to test if it rains, and then steps inside again.)*

*(Enter **MARIANNE**, walking with the support of **ELINOR**.)*

MARIANNE. There, exactly there, on that projecting mound, there I fell; and there I first saw Willoughby.

>*(Pause.)*

I am not wishing him too much good, when I wish his secret reflections may be no more unpleasant than my own.

ELINOR. Do you compare your conduct with his?

MARIANNE. No. I compare it with what it ought to have been. I compare it with yours.

>*(**ELINOR** presses her hand.)*

>*(A pause.)*

My illness has made me think. Long before I was enough recovered to talk, I was perfectly able to reflect. Whenever I looked towards the past, I saw some duty neglected, or some failing indulged. Everybody seemed injured by me. The kindness, the unceasing kindness of Mrs. Jennings, I had repaid with ungrateful contempt. But it is my sister that I have most offended.

ELINOR. Dearest, do not reproach yourself further. Any fault you have committed against me is freely forgiven. I am so glad to see you well again.

MARIANNE. You are very good.

(*Enter* **MRS. DASHWOOD.**)

MRS. DASHWOOD. Do not linger too long, my dear – the air is damp. You must not catch a chill.

MARIANNE. Have no fears of that, Mama. I mean in future to do nothing but that which is most conducive to my health, and to the comfort of those I love. My feelings shall be governed and my temper improved. They shall no longer worry others, nor torture myself. I shall now live solely for my family. You and Elinor must henceforth be all the world to me. As for Willoughby, I cannot say that I shall soon, or that I shall ever, forget him, but I shall regard him only as a bad memory.

(*Exit* **MRS. DASHWOOD** *and* **MARIANNE.**)

(**ELINOR** *goes to follow, but then:*)

(*Enter* **MRS. JENNINGS.**)

MRS. JENNINGS. Good morning, Miss Dashwood, good morning. And how is your sister, my dear?

ELINOR. Much, much better, thank you.

MRS. JENNINGS. And have you heard the news? About our Lucy?

ELINOR. I own I have not.

MRS. JENNINGS. Oh, such a going on, my dear. But we have news at last – my manservant, Henry, tells me that she is married – married to Mr. Ferrars.

ELINOR. Married?

MRS. JENNINGS. Henry saw them himself, this very day. They were stopping in a carriage at the door of the New London Inn. He happened to look up as they went by in the carriage, and so saw directly that it was Lucy Steele.

ELINOR. And she was married?

MRS. JENNINGS. So it seems – she told Henry she had changed her name since she was last in these parts, and is now Mrs. Ferrars. So they are wed at last, the poor souls! Well, I wish them joy. And now I must go and pay my respects to your mother.

(She exits. **ELINOR** *sinks onto a stool.)*

(Enter **MARIANNE**, *who sits beside her and, in an obvious reversal of roles, comforts her by taking her hand. Another pause. Enter* **EDWARD**.)

MARIANNE. *(Starting up.)* Edward!

ELINOR. *(Resignedly.)* Edward.

> **(EDWARD** *takes* **MARIANNE**'s *offered hand, and then waits in uncomfortable silence.)*

MARIANNE. Very – dry, the weather has been recently... quite pleasant for the time of year...wouldn't you say?

EDWARD. Yes...very.

ELINOR. Is Mrs. Ferrars staying nearby?

EDWARD. Nearby! No, my mother is in town.

ELINOR. I meant to enquire for Mrs. Edward Ferrars.

EDWARD. Perhaps you mean – my brother – you mean Mrs....Mrs. *Robert* Ferrars.

MARIANNE. Mrs. Robert Ferrars!

EDWARD. Perhaps you do not know that – you may not have heard that my brother Robert is lately married to...to Miss Lucy Steele.

> **(ELINOR** *stands in astonishment.)*

ELINOR. Then, you are not married?

EDWARD. No.

MARIANNE. Oh Edward!

> **(MARIANNE** *darts from the room, leaving* **EDWARD** *and her sister alone.)*

EDWARD. Elinor, I met Lucy when I was very young. I made a great mistake in becoming attached to her. Then, when I met you, I was simple enough to think, that because my faith was plighted to another, there could be no danger in my being with you. I felt that I admired you, but I told myself it was only friendship; when I found I loved you, I told myself the danger was my own. I have stayed away to try to lessen that love, I have avoided you to try to cease to think of you, but to no avail. I knew that my duty was to stand by Lucy as long as she loved me. I could not abandon her when she was prepared to face trouble for me, to undergo hardship and to suffer for me. Then, when my mother saw fit to disinherit me, Lucy called our engagement off, and my brother Robert, who had spent so much time with her in the hope of persuading her to relinquish her attachment, succeeded more completely than he had ever imagined, in transferring her attachment to himself.

ELINOR. And Lucy is – is married to Robert?

EDWARD. Yes. Lucy is married, and I am finally at liberty to say to you what I have wanted to say for so long. I come here with no expectations. As you know, I have no fortune, nothing to offer you. I come only to profess, now that I am at liberty to do so, how utterly I love you.

(**ELINOR** *is weeping and laughing at once.*)

ELINOR. Oh, Edward!

(**EDWARD** *takes her hand, and gets down on one knee.*)

EDWARD. Miss Dashwood – Elinor – dearest Elinor – after all that has passed, is there a chance you might consider – could it be possible – will you be my wife?

ELINOR. Darling Edward, yes! I am yours. I am yours.

(*They embrace.*)

You will think me sentimental, but I do not care. You have made me happier than I ever thought I could be.

(*They kiss.*)

EDWARD. It may be a short while until we can marry. As you know, my mother has disinherited me, and has left me little enough to live upon. But I shall have employment soon. When Colonel Brandon learned that my mother had cast me off for standing by my engagement to Lucy, he offered me a living as a clergyman on his estate at Delaford.

ELINOR. Edward, this is wonderful!

EDWARD. I know I must owe this entirely to your kindness.

ELINOR. You owe it entirely to your own goodness – the Colonel has often spoken highly of you, and it is from his regard that this must proceed. I have had no hand in this, or knowledge of it.

EDWARD. Of course, the Colonel offered it, believing that it would enable me to marry *Lucy*. He may be a little surprised at the change of circumstances.

ELINOR. I must confess myself astonished that Lucy has released you from your engagement; she professed herself to be so very much in love with you – and so suddenly, to marry your brother!

EDWARD. I share your astonishment. It seems her feelings altered, and I have Lucy's own words to explain it – she sent me a letter on the day of her elopement.

> (*He takes out the letter and hands it to* **ELINOR**, *who reads it.*)

[MUSIC CUE "LUCY'S LETTER"]

> (*Enter* **LUCY**, *above.*)

LUCY. Dear Sir, Being very sure I have long lost your affections, I have thought myself at liberty to bestow my own on another, for I scorned to accept a hand while the heart was another's. I sincerely wish you happy in your choice, and it shall not be my fault if we are not always good friends. I can safely say I owe you no ill will, and am sure you will be too generous to do us any ill offices. Your brother has gained my affections entirely, and as we could not live without one another, we are just returned from the altar, and I thought I would trouble you with these few lines. I shall always remain your sincere well-wisher, friend, and sister, Lucy Ferrars.

P.S. I have burnt all your letters, and will return your picture with the first opportunity. Please do destroy my scrawls; but the ring, with my hair, you are welcome to keep.

> (*Exit* **LUCY**.)

> (**ELINOR** *returns the letter.*)

EDWARD. I will not ask your opinion of it. Since the first half-year of our foolish – business – this is the only letter I ever received from her that has given me any joy.

ELINOR. Just now, I am in the mood to forgive Lucy anything.

> (*They embrace.*)

> (*Enter* **MRS. DASHWOOD**, *closely followed by* **MARIANNE**.)

MRS. DASHWOOD. I cannot wait a moment longer!

MARIANNE. (*Laughing.*) Mama!

MRS. DASHWOOD. Tell me, is it settled? Are you to be married?

ELINOR. We are, Mama.

EDWARD. Elinor has accepted me.

MRS. DASHWOOD. Then I may do what I have long wished to do, Edward, and welcome you as a son.

> (*She embraces him;* **MARIANNE** *and* **ELINOR** *embrace, then* **MARIANNE** *reaches out to embrace* **EDWARD** *–*)

MARIANNE. Dearest Edward!

> (*– And leads him into the house, while* **MRS. DASHWOOD** *and* **ELINOR** *embrace.*)

MRS. DASHWOOD. I wish you very happy, my dear girl.

ELINOR. (*Moved.*) Thank you, Mama.

> (*Exit* **MRS. DASHWOOD** *and* **ELINOR** *after them.*)

Scene Four

[MUSIC CUE "THE JOYS OF THE COUNTRY"]

(Time passes.)

(Enter **ELINOR**, **EDWARD**, **MARIANNE**, *and* **BRANDON**, *with picnic things.)*

(They sit, and begin to read aloud from The Dramatic Writings of Shakespeare – *with* **BRANDON** *and* **MARIANNE** *reading, and the others watching.* **ELINOR** *sketches the pair as they read and hands the pad to* **EDWARD**, *who also attempts an outline. A mood of celebration, and of familiarity, prevails – this is one of many summer afternoons where they have sat and read together.* **BRANDON** *and* **MARIANNE** *are closer than before, and are easy and comfortable with one another as they read.)*

MARIANNE. *(As Viola.)* But if she cannot love you, sir?

BRANDON. *(As Orsino.)* I cannot be so answered.

MARIANNE. *(As Viola.)* Sooth, but you must.
Say that some lady, as perhaps there is,
Hath for your love as great a pang of heart
As you have for Olivia. You cannot love her.
You tell her so. Must she not then be answered?

BRANDON. *(As Orsino.)* There is no woman's sides
Can bide the beating of so strong a passion
As love doth give my heart. No woman's heart
So big, to hold so much. They lack retention.
Alas, their love may be called appetite –

> *(He looks at* **MRS. DASHWOOD** *at this moment, who enters with a tray of cakes, prompting much laughter among the others.)*

No motion of the liver, but the palate,

That suffer surfeit, cloyment, and revolt.
But mine is all as hungry as the sea –

> *(He pops a cake into his mouth.)*

And can digest as much.

> *(They laugh as he chews and swallows.)*

Make no compare
Between that love a woman can bear me
And that I owe Olivia.

MARIANNE. *(As Viola.)* Ay, but I know –

BRANDON. *(As Orsino.)* What dost thou know?

MARIANNE. *(As Viola, but with great sincerity.)* Too well what love women to men may owe.
In faith, they are as true of heart as we.
My father had a daughter loved a man
As it might be perhaps, were I a woman,
I should your lordship.

> *(They look at one another. **BRANDON**, instead of replying, takes her hand and gently kisses it.)*

(Blushing.) No, no, he does not relent yet! He does not know she is a woman – he still believes she is a boy.

BRANDON. Then Orsino is a fool.

> *(All laugh.)*

EDWARD. Let us not be too hard on Orsino. He believes himself in love with one woman, and is unprepared to fall in love with another...disguised as his pageboy.

MARIANNE. We shall never get through *Twelfth Night* if Orsino persists in trying to declare his affections to Viola!

BRANDON. *(Playful.)* I will endeavour to restrain myself, Marianne.

ELINOR. What do you say to second attachments now, Marianne? Is Shakespeare mistaken again?

MARIANNE. *(Smiling shyly at* **BRANDON.***)* I believe there is something to be said in favour of second chances.

(Curtain.)

[MUSIC CUE "PARTING GLASS"]

Milton Keynes UK
Ingram Content Group UK Ltd.
UKHW020625100524
442500UK00010B/90